THE
HOOLIGANS

By

Tom Townsend

EAKIN PRESS ★ Austin, Texas

Library of Congress Cataloging-in-Publication Data

Townsend, Tom.
    The hooligans / by Tom Townsend.
        p.   cm.
    Summary: Eager to take part in the war effort, a group of orphans run
away from their orphanage and become crew for a schooner patrolling the
Atlantic for Nazi submarines.
    ISBN 0-89015-792-8 : $9.95
    [1. World War, 1939–1945 — Naval operations — Fiction. 2. Orphans —
Fiction. 3. Sea stories.] I. Title.
PZ7.T666Ho   1990
[Fic.]--dc 20
                                          90-43149
                                            CIP
                                            AC

FIRST EDITION

Published in the United States of America
By Eakin Press
An Imprint of Eakin Publications, Inc.
P.O. Drawer 90159 ★ Austin, TX 78709-0159

ISBN 0-89015-792-8

Illustrations by Peter Cuthbert
Cover illustration by Peter Cuthbert

For Rufus G. "Bud" Smith,
who told me about the sailing yachts
that went to war.

1

"The penguins are gonna catch you," Slug McDermitt whispered as he sat on his bed and watched Butch Hoover tear his mattress cover into strips.

"Ain't nobody gonna catch me, not never," Butch swore.

Slug let out a gurgling laugh that made the fat on his belly ripple like soft Jell-o. "They got ya last time before ya got over the fence. Tanned yer hide real good."

"Shut up!"

Feet shuffled, and a small, freckled face peeked up over the bed. "Wish't I was goin' wit ya," Tadpole Wilson said.

"Yer too little," Butch told him as he tied another two strips of mattress cover together and pulled the knot tight. "I'm gonna be movin' real fast, and I gotta travel light," he added, trying to sound tough. "But someday, I'll figure out a way to come back for you. Maybe when the war's over. Deal?"

"Yeah, Butch. Deal!"

"They ain't gonna let you join no navy. Navy don't take nobody that's only thirteen." It was a dark-complexioned kid with shifty eyes, called Cockroach, who spoke.

"Oh, yeah? We'll see," Butch replied as he stood up to open the narrow, third-floor window. "I'm big for my age." The window creaked as he raised it. "But, no matter what, I ain't stayin' in this stinkin' orphanage no longer."

"Got a lock-pick I'll sell ya for a quarter," Cockroach said. "You gotta steal to make it on the streets."

"Get outta here." Butch made a threatening move toward Cockroach.

"Yeah, scram," Slug added, and screwed his lopsided face into a threatening sneer. No one liked Cockroach.

"Rat-ta-tat, rat-ta-tat, rat-ta-tat, voom voom, splut, splut, splut!"

"Gunner, be quiet! Ya wanna wake the penguins?" Butch whispered loudly at a skinny boy with rather long, straight hair, who had just soared down an aisle between the line of beds and landed noisily on the floor.

"Sparks says he's ready. Gonna knock out the lights when you give the word," Gunner announced.

"Yeah, good, but you gotta be quiet!"

For as long as anyone could remember, Gunner Yeats always pretended to be an airplane. Everywhere he went, he revved up his imaginary engine, spread his arms like wings, and soared around the orphanage, making banking turns in the hall and dive-bombing down the stairs. Now he folded his arms like a Corsair returned to the deck of an aircraft carrier, and sat quietly.

Butch finished tying his mattress cover rope around a heater that never worked. He looked out of the window at the ground, three stories below. There were floodlights on each corner of the building, and at the edge of their yellowish light he could just make out the shadows of a swingset and a slide. Beyond them, he knew, was a high fence and then . . . He gulped, took a deep breath, and told himself once again that this was the only way.

2

"You sure Sparks can put all the lights out?" he nervously asked Gunner.

The airplane shrugged. "That's what he says. You know Sparks — nutty as a fruitcake. He's got two big wires stuck in the wall socket. Says all he has to do is touch 'em to one of the iron heaters."

"Fruitcake . . ." Slug moaned. "I could eat a dozen of 'em."

"You could eat a dozen anything," Butch said. "Now hand me my bag." An old potato sack was placed in Butch's hand. He took another deep breath. "Okay, Gunner, tell 'em I'm ready."

"Switch on. Contact," Gunner said, and again the imaginary airplane sputtered to life and soared off toward the far end of the dormitory room.

Butch turned back to Slug and Tadpole. "You guys take care of yourselves now, an' don't take no lip from the penguins."

"Kill some Germans for me — or some Japs," Tadpole said.

Butch started to say good-bye just as a fountain of brilliant blue sparks erupted at the far end of the room. Lightning-like flashes danced on the walls as other boys dove for cover. Then there was silence and total darkness. Butch dropped his sack out the window, took hold of his rope, and started down.

His feet slipped on the damp, brick wall as he passed the second-story window. That floor was the girls' dormitory and inside he could hear screaming and laughing. Too late, he noticed that the window was open.

"Where ya think ya goin', Butch?" a high-pitched, girl's voice asked.

Butch stared up into the face of Maisy Martin. Her blue eyes and turned-up nose were framed with frizzy blond hair. "I'm bustin' out, now be quiet!"

"I want ta go too!" Maisy whispered loudly.

"Ain't no way I'm takin' along some dumb girl," Butch said and lowered himself to the first-floor win-

3

dows. There, he hung motionless for a few moments as a candle flickered from inside. In its light, he could see two of the matrons who were in charge of the orphanage. They seemed to be trying to make a lamp work. Both of them were dressed in their usual drab, black-and-white uniforms.

They really do look like penguins, Butch thought, cautiously easing himself to the ground.

A cool east wind blew off the ocean and combed his red hair. He could hear waves breaking beneath the cliffs less than a mile away. Butch grabbed up his sack and ran through the playground. Like a cat, he climbed the high fence beyond and used his bag to cover the three strands of barbed wire at its top. On the other side, he hit the ground running and did not stop until he was at the edge of the bluffs. Behind him, the dark walls of the Greystone State Orphanage sat glowering in the night like an unhappy troll. Before him was the sea, where white-capped breakers marched in toward the shore and exploded into giant clouds of flying spray.

Perhaps it was the sea which called to him, as much as the war. Memories of his father's skipjack, dredging oysters on Chesapeake Bay, were like old, faded photographs lurking on the distant fringes of his mind's eye. *It all must have been a very long time ago,* he thought.

Fire was on the far horizon — a distant, red-orange glow, somewhere out beyond the tip of Cape Hatteras. "U-boats got another one," he said to himself and started walking along the cliff.

It had been two months before — February of 1942 — that he had seen the first distant fire which marked the position of a burning American ship. Since then, it happened almost every night. How could he — how could anyone — be expected to sit there in that miserable orphanage and watch enemy submarines sink American ships within sight of the coast? Somehow, he had to do something. Somehow, he had to go to war.

4

2

Old Commodore Winston Merriweather puffed thought-fully on his pipe and "huffed" as he surveyed the gray-painted schooner on the drydock. "*Southwind* looks a mite different, all painted up like a warship," he said.

"Actually, Grandfather, she looks quite ugly, and not fit to be seen at the yacht club," answered fourteen-year-old Stanley Merriweather, as he sat on a piling.

"Humph," Merriweather returned. "Well, when this blasted war is over with, we'll have her painted white again and all the brightwork shined up. But for now, *Southwind* has other work to do, and we don't want some Nazi U-boat spotting a white hull and polished brass." He puffed again on his pipe, and circles of smoke curled around his gray hair. "But, camouflage gray or snow white, she's still a lady, and still just as fast as she was the day she won the Bermuda Race two years ago."

The schooner *Southwind* was a little over one hundred feet long from the tip of her bowsprit to the rail on her wineglass-shaped stern, where her tender hung

5

from a pair of davits. Her two masts were raked back at a jaunty angle and were so tall that they seemed to reach almost to the sky. For as long as Stanley could remember, *Southwind* had been the flagship of the Sandy Shores Yacht Club. Grandfather Merriweather had been commodore there for almost as long.

"Not many schooners like her left," old Merriweather said, as he had said many times before. "It will feel good to get her back to sea again."

Stanley stood up and brushed a bit of shipyard dust off his blue short pants. He buttoned his matching school blazer and straightened his tie. "Grandmama says that you are too old to be sailing off to war again."

Merriweather laughed, and then coughed. "Does she now? As I remember it, she said I was too old to go sailing off to the First World War, but I went anyway. Besides, standing picket duty on a sailing yacht is hardly like 'going off to war.' All *Southwind* has to do is patrol the coast and help out the Coast Guard for a few months."

Stanley kicked at a rock and scuffed the polished toe of his shoe. "I really don't understand what the Coast Guard expects to accomplish with sailboats," he said.

Again, Merriweather huffed. "Well, the truth is, this whole idea was cooked up by some fellows up at the New York Yacht Club. They've put a whole squadron together up there."

"And we are suppossed to search for enemy submarines?" Stanley asked doubtfully.

Merriweather nodded. "Yes. It's no secret that ever since we got into this war, those German U-boats have been sinking ships all along our coast. Our Coast Guard and the navy needs more time to get enough ships together to deal with them. So until they do, some of us yachtsmen are going to give them a hand."

"That's all well and good, Grandfather. But why have they chosen to use sailboats? They are terribly slow,

6

and there are so many fast power cruisers around nowadays."

Merriweather leaned on his cane and laughed. "Ah, but the navy recently discovered that these old, slow sailboats have a special advantage for finding submarines."

"Whatever could that be?"

"Well, you see, submarines use a special electronic device called 'sonar.' It can hear a ship's engine miles away, and even tell them which direction to go to find it." He pointed with his pipe at the drydock. "Now, *Southwind* there doesn't have any need to use her engine when she's at sea, and so they don't know we're around."

Stanley scratched his head. "But how are we supposed to know when a submarine is around?"

"We will have a device that listens to their motors. Don't ask me how it works; it's just one of those newfangled machines the government is coming up with all the time."

Stanley frowned thoughtfully. "And so, when we hear a submarine, we call the navy on our radio, and they come out and sink it?"

"Exactly," Merriweather nodded. "At least that is the plan, and so far, it's the best one we have."

Stanley sighed. "I suppose it might work — that is, if we can find a crew somewhere. I'm afraid that everyone who's old enough has either joined the army or the navy. It doesn't seem like there is anyone left to crew a sailboat."

Old Merriweather tried to look confident. "I've let it be known about that I'm looking for a crew for *Southwind*. We should turn out a few able hands."

"Perhaps I can stay on after summer vacation," Stanley said carefully.

Merriweather continued to stare at the schooner. "You could, except, of course, your mother would never allow it. It's hard to believe she let you go for the summer." He looked seriously at Stanley for a moment. "Cer-

7

tainly was convenient how your school let out early this year."

"Yes, yes it was," Stanley said, and quickly changed the subject. "Well, whatever happens, I've got at least the next three months. By then, well, who knows?"

"Yes," Merriweather said and rose stiffly to his feet. "For now, there's plenty of work you can help me with, just getting *Southwind* ready to sail," he said and strode off toward the drydock.

When the commodore was gone, Stanley reached into the pocket of his blazer and removed a letter he had stolen from the mailbox only that morning. For a while, he stared at the envelope and felt sick. The return address was "Briar Gate Boarding School — his school. Once again, he took out the letter, and read,

Dear Mr. & Mrs. Merriweather,
    I regret to inform you that your son Stanley has been dismisssed from this institution. He was found to be cheating on his semester tests.

There was no need to read further. He hid the letter back in his pocket and followed his grandfather toward the schooner. Stanley knew that they would all find out sooner or later. But if *Southwind* could be gotten to sea soon enough, then at least he would have the summer before he would have to face them. By then — well, that was a long way off.

The chief petty officer at the Coast Guard recruiting station seemed to be about seven feet tall and almost as wide. A heart and the word "Mother" were tattooed on one bulging muscle of his left arm. On his right were an anchor and crossed cannons. He peered suspiciously over the top of his desk, bit down on the end of a half-smoked cigar, and squinted one eye. "Wadda ya want?" he growled at the boy who had just entered his office.

8

"I want to join the Coast Guard, sir."

"Who are you?"

"Name's Butch Hoover, sir. I . . ."

With one hairy hand, the chief took his cigar out of his mouth and leaned closer to the boy. "Now just how old am I supposed ta believe you are?"

"Eighteen, sir," Butch recited his well-practiced lie, which in the past week had failed to impress the navy, Marine Corps, the army, and the Army Air Corps.

"Eighteen?" the chief repeated through gritted teeth. "Eighteen what? Months, weeks, days? Certainly not years."

"I — I'm just a little small for my age. I graduated from school last year."

The chief nodded slowly. "And of course you've got your birth certificate and your diploma with you."

"Well, no sir. Truth is, they got all burned up when our house caught fire last month, and — "

"Get outa here!" the chief yelled, pointing his finger at the door.

Butch wilted. The Coast Guard had been his last hope, and he had failed here too. "Aw heck," he sighed. "Ain't there nothin' I can do ta help out in this war?"

For several long moments, the chief sat silently chewing his cigar. "You ever been on a boat?" he asked finally.

Butch nodded. "My dad owned a skipjack, dredging oysters. I worked with him all the time — 'till he took sick an' died." Feeling a tear begin to well up in one eye, he turned to leave.

He was halfway to the door when the chief stopped him. Without looking up from a paper he was reading, he asked, "You know what a schooner is?"

Butch turned slowly, not understanding why he would ask. "Yes, sir, I seen a few of 'em."

"Pier five, she's called the *Southwind*. See Commodore Merriweather." It took Butch a moment to realize

Finding your way around the Southwind

1. *Engine*
2. *Bowsprit*
3. *Crew's Quarters*
4. *Galley*
5. *Guest Cabins*
6. *Main Hatch*
7. *Wheel*
8. *Radio Room*
9. *Main Salon*

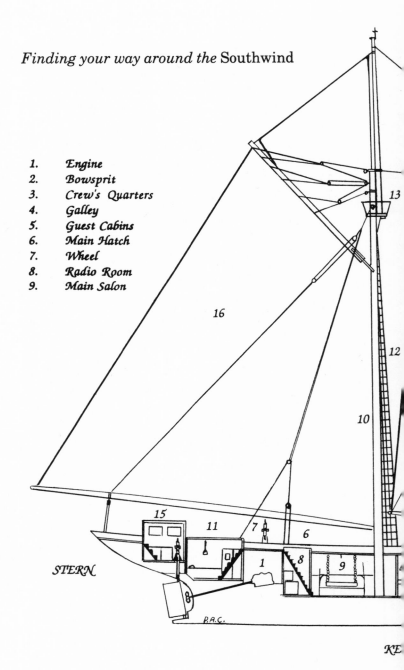

STERN

P.A.C.

KE

10

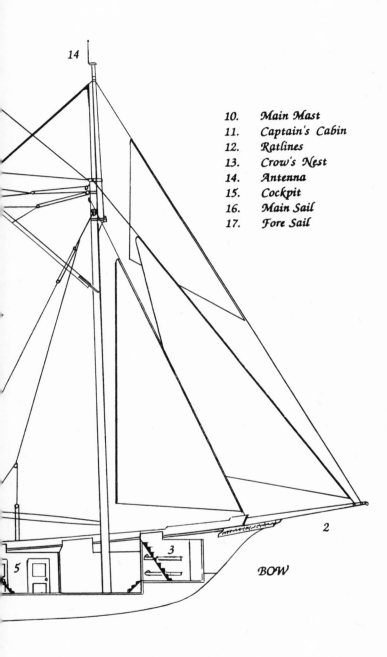

14

10. Main Mast
11. Captain's Cabin
12. Ratlines
13. Crow's Nest
14. Antenna
15. Cockpit
16. Main Sail
17. Fore Sail

2

3

5

BOW

what he was saying. His mouth opened to say "thanks," but the chief frowned and pointed his cigar at him. "And you don't tell nobody nothin' about who sent you. 'Cause if you do, I'll come lookin' for you and turn you inside out."

"Yessir, thank you, sir," Butch blurted out and ran for the door.

The chief watched him go and then reread the paper in his hand.

To: COMMANDING OFFICER; U.S. COAST GUARD RECRUITING OFFICE
Subject: Runaway child
Local police request you be on lookout for Butch Hoover, age 13. Red hair, 5'1" tall. Recently escaped from Greystone State Home For Delinquent Children. Has been seen in your area and has made numerous attempts to join other branches of armed services.

The chief shook his head. "Greystone, that's where they keep all the ones that got screws loose," he said as he wadded up the paper. "I might be makin' a really big mistake, but I probably wouldn't sleep nights if I turned him in." He tossed the paper into the nearest wastebasket and started looking for a match to relight his cigar.

3

A light rain was falling and fog had rolled in off the Atlantic Ocean when Butch finally found Pier 5.

Don't see nothin' that looks like a schooner out there, he thought. He threw his sack over his shoulder and started walking down the pier anyway. Gray-painted patrol boats with white numbers on their bows were moored along one side. Smoke curled from all four stacks of a two-hundred-foot navy destroyer/escort, which took up most of the other side. Everywhere there were sailors who all seemed to be in a hurry. *That's okay,* Butch thought. *There's a war on . . . I'm in a hurry too.*

He was surprised to find the *Southwind* moored at the very end of the pier, hidden by the destroyer's towering stern. For a while he stood admiring her sleek lines and gazing up at her tall, pointed masts. They were, he guessed, nearly twice as high as most of the skipjacks he had seen. Through one of her cabin ports a light was shining, so he called out in his deepest voice. "Hello aboard!" The head and shoulders of a well-dressed boy about his own age appeared suddenly at the hatch.

"I'm here to see Commodore Merriweather," Butch announced.

The other boy stared at him for a long moment, running his eyes disdainfully over his ragged clothes and dirty face. "I suppose you must be one of the new crewmen," the boy said.

"Uh, yes, sir. Name's Hoover, Butch Hoover," Butch answered, thinking fast.

The boy hesitated. "I was expecting someone older, actually. But I suppose you are all they could find."

"I'm real small for my age — fools people all the time."

"Well, come aboard then," the boy said in a disappointed tone. "I am Stanley Merriweather, the commodore's grandson. For the moment I am in charge. And by the way, it is not 'Commodore Merriweather' anymore. He will be addressed by you as 'Captain,' of course." Again Butch found himself being inspected. "My word, you look as though the cat has been dragging you around."

Butch managed to hold his temper. "Yeah, well, I been travelin' for a week or so," he explained, "ever since I left my last ship."

Stanley led him down a few short steps to the schooner's main salon. Here, everything was beautiful shades of polished and varnished wood. A long table was suspended from the overhead on chains so that it would always remain level, even when the ship was rolling in a stormy sea. There were soft, cushioned settees, and shiny brass lamps, which cast a warm glow over the wood.

"Come along," Stanley ordered. "You may stow your gear in the crew's quarters, forward."

From the salon, they passed into the galley, where coals glowed from inside a heavy cookstove and plates were secured neatly on shelves with little railings. The odor of beef stew hit Butch like a big rock, reminding him painfully that he had not eaten for a day.

"My grandmother sent some stew and biscuits down for lunch. It's on the stove there," Stanley said casually, "but of course it's after two, so you would have eaten already."

"Uh, well — yes, of course, I have," Butch managed, but slipped a biscuit into his pocket as he passed the stove.

The passageway continued past two other doors which Butch was told led to private cabins for guests. At the end of the passage, Stanley opened a door marked "crew's quarters." Inside were four narrow bunks built into the wall and four small lockers. A table took up most of the floor space, and a single kerosene lamp hung above it. Butch compared it to the orphanage, and decided it looked wonderful.

"Since you seem to be the first man to arrive, you have your choice of bunks," Stanley continued. "I do hope the others get here soon. There is so much work to do before we sail."

"How soon is that?"

Stanley shook his head. "That is a military secret. Even I don't know." Immediately he changed the subject. "Put up your gear and meet me on deck. There is a lot of equipment coming aboard this afternoon that will need stowing."

Stanley left, and Butch wilted against one on the bunks and ate his stolen biscuit. He simply could not believe his good fortune. He had actually gotten himself aboard a warship, even if it was only an old wooden schooner. Now all he had to do was hang on and not let anyone know how old he was until they sailed. Then it would be too late for anyone to stop him.

An hour later, strange-looking crates began to arrive on deck. They came out of the back of a navy truck which drove up the pier, and several sailors carried them onto

Southwind's deck. Stanley signed an official-looking piece of paper, and the sailors left.

"What's all this stuff?" Butch asked, as he stood on deck in the rain.

"Electronic equipment, radios and — this one says it's a 'magnetometer'. You know what that is?"

"Nope." Butch shrugged.

"That's for our radio operator to deal with, whenever Grandfather finds one," Stanley said. "Just carry everything down below for now."

Several of the boxes were much too big for Butch to carry by himself and, much to Stanley's dislike, he found himself having to help. By the time they had finished, both boys were tired and wet.

Stanley looked at his small, gold pocket watch. "I really thought Grandfather would be here with the rest of our crew by now. I can't understand what could be keeping them."

As it turned out, darkness had already come when Captain Merriweather stepped down through the hatch, with rain dripping from the brim of his yachting cap. "Ah, Grandfather," Stanley greeted him. "We've been wondering where you were."

"Out trying to turn up some crew, my boy," Merriweather began. "Seems like everyone who is able has already joined some other service."

"I thought some of your chums from the yacht club would jump at a chance to sail with you again."

"Most of them have already signed on one of the other yachts," Merriweather said sadly. "Did you know that *Caribee* and *Windrose* are also fitting out? Seems they've beat us to most of the good hands." At last he noticed Butch. "And who have we here?"

"Name's Butch . . . Butch Hoover. I'm here ta crew for you."

Merriweather squinted his eyes and frowned. "How old are you?"

16

"Eighteen, sir."

"Eighteen," Merriweather repeated doubtfully.

"He's small for his age," Stanley chimed in.

Merriweather pulled off his raincoat and poured himself a cup of tea in the galley. "Well, lads, it is beginning to look as though we won't be sailing at all," he said with disappointment slipping into his voice. "There is simply no one left on the docks to sail *Southwind*."

"But that is terrible, Grandfather," Stanley said loudly. "There must be some way . . ."

"If there is, I certainly do not know what it is."

" 'Scuse me, sir," Butch ventured. "About how many hands would you need?"

Merriweather began to count on his fingers. "We'll need a radio operator who knows something about those newfangled listening devices. And a good seacook. We might get by with three hands per watch, I suppose. Why, lad? Do you know where we might find some?"

"Well, sir . . ." Butch hesitated. The plan that was just beginning to take shape in his mind was still not thought out enough to try to explain. "No, I was just wonderin'."

Merriweather looked at his watch. "I am late for dinner," he noted. "Stanley, are you coming with me?"

Stanley was looking strangely at Butch. "Uh, no sir," he said. "I think I shall spend the night aboard, in case anyone else shows up to join the crew. It's all right. I've told Mother."

As soon as Merriweather had left, Stanley turned back to Butch. "You know where we can find a crew, don't you?"

"Maybe," Butch shrugged. "But they probably wouldn't be the kind you want."

Stanley rose and began to pace back and forth between the table and the hatchway. "Look, Hoover, I'm going to level with you. Grandfather really wants to do his part in this war. It's important to him and, well, it's

17

important to me too, for my own reasons." He reached onto a shelf and picked up some pieces of paper.

Butch found himself fidgeting nervously as Stanley talked. Things were moving too fast. If he told Stanley what he was thinking, he would have to admit to running away from the orphanage. That could ruin everything.

Suddenly, Stanley dropped the paper in front of him. Butch started to read it and got as far as "escaped from Greystone State Home For . . ."

"If you know where we can find some men, you'd better tell me," Stanley threatened as he put both hands on the table, narrowed his eyes, and stared straight at Butch. "Because if you don't, I'll call the police and have you sent back to that stinking orphanage you ran away from last week!"

4

"I didn't do nothin', but nothin'!" Slug McDermitt cried as Matron Grabouski dragged him out of the dining hall. "I don't know nothin', I ain't never knowed nothin', an' I don't wanna know nothin'!"

"I did not say that you knew anything. I said the sheriff is on the telephone and wants to talk to you about Butch Hoover," Matron Grabouski insisted as she opened the office door, released her grip on the collar of his shirt, and pointed toward the telephone on the wall. Slug took a few uncertain steps toward the phone. He wiped his nose on his sleeve, picked up the receiver, and burped.

"Slug, that you?" The voice did not sound like a sheriff.

"Yeah, who is — "

"Shut up and listen. It's me . . . Butch."

"Ha, ha, I told you they'd catch — "

"I said shut up an' listen, ya dumb ox! Now, just answer 'yes' or 'no.' Ya got that?" Butch said.

"Yeah, Butch — "

"Don't say my name! Just pretend you're talkin' to the sheriff."

"Yeah, okay," Slug answered. "So how ya doin' there, Sheriff ol' buddy?"

"Shut up! I'm bustin' you guys out tonight. You get the word to Sparks, an' Gunner, an' any of the other big guys who wanna go, 'cept Cockroach. He'd just be trouble. I can take six of you, no more. Ya got that?"

"Yeah, uh — Sheriff. I got that."

Butch breathed a little sigh of relief. So far, so good. "Okay, now, ya tell 'em to be ready at midnight. And see if Sparks can knock out the lights again."

"Okay, Sheriff," Slug said as he cast a quick glance over his shoulder to see where Matron Grabouski was. "Uh, where we goin' to?" he asked in a whisper.

"Tell 'em they're joinin' the Coast Guards, to go fight Germans," Butch said, knowing that most of it was a lie. "Remember, midnight!" he added.

"Yeah, well, good-bye there, Sheriff. Like I tol' ya, I don't know nothin', and I never did know nothin' and fact is I never really wanted to know nothin' . . ."

Butch hung up the phone and turned to Stanley, who was standing beside him in the shipyard office at the end of Pier 5. "It's set," he said. "Now you want ta tell me how we're gonna get all the way over to Greystone?"

Stanley thought for a moment. "We may have to steal a car," he suggested.

Butch had been considering the same thing but had been afraid to suggest it, mostly because he was afraid Stanley would like the idea. "I was hopin' there was some other way. I got caught stealin' a couple of times already. If they get me again, it's 'the big house' for sure."

Stanley yawned and stared out the window. "That is true, but if I turn you in for running off, you'll probably end up there anyway. So the way I see it, you really don't have much to lose by doing things my way."

Butch fought down the sudden urge to put his fist in

Stanley's mouth. He walked to the window and looked out at a little open vehicle painted navy gray. "You know how to drive?" he asked.

"I've driven the family Duesenberg, several times. That thing couldn't possibly be as hard as that."

"What is it? It looks too small to be a truck."

"That is a totally new type of vehicle — a Willys quarter-ton truck, only now I hear they call it a 'jeep'."

"Jeep? That's a dumb name!"

"Perhaps. It's named after that character in the Popeye cartoon strip, you know, the one that just says 'jeep, jeep, jeep' all the time."

"Well, whatever they call it, don't ya think the navy is gonna be mad when they find it gone?"

"Not if it's back by morning," Stanley assured him. "My only question is, is it big enough for all the boys and their luggage?"

Butch laughed bitterly. "Those guys ain't got no luggage. They barely got the clothes on their backs."

Stanley raised one eyebrow. "Really? Well, that settles it then. Let's go."

Outside in the rain, Stanley managed to get the jeep started without too much trouble. "Don't it need a key?" Butch asked.

"Of course not. If the navy had trucks with keys, the sailors would lose them all. This one just has a simple switch," Stanley explained as he ground the gears, trying to get the jeep moving. By accident, he found reverse and backed over a couple of garbage cans behind the office. For a while, forward eluded him as gears ground and the engine revved. At last the little vehicle shot forward, and Butch was barely able to hang on as they drove out the gate and onto the street in a series of short jerks.

"Hey! I thought you told me you knew how to drive!" Butch yelled as Stanley ran up onto a curb and barely got back on the road without hitting a mailbox.

21

Stephen Jones liked his nickname "Sparks." It had been given to him by the other boys at Greystone after he had blown the windows out of the restroom with a home-made bomb assembled from garden fertilizer, matches, and an entire roll of toilet paper. Sparks was not a very big boy, and the other kids used to call him "Four Eyes" because of the thick, horn-rimmed glasses he had to wear in order to read. And reading was very important to Sparks. Reading was how he learned to make bombs, short out electrical circuits, and do all the other stuff he was good at.

"Hey, Sparks," Slug said and bounced on his bed. "You ready to hit 'em?"

Sparks was busy packing. "Yeah, I'm ready. Ol' Sparks is always ready," he said as he stuffed the last of his collection of back issues of *Science and Mechanics* magazine into his pillowcase.

"What ya takin' them for?" Slug asked.

"Because they're mine," Sparks said as he threw in his spare underwear. "An' besides, I might need 'em ta help us sink Nazi ships."

"Yeah?"

"Yeah, Slug, we might need 'em," Sparks repeated. With Slug, you usually had to say things twice. He tied a knot in the pillowcase, then reached under his mattress and pulled out two long pieces of electrical wire. With practiced ease, he wrapped the bare ends around two of the iron heaters and took the other ends to a wall socket. "Just tell me when," he said.

Across the room, Tadpole was putting on his shoes and having a hard time tying the laces. "He going too?" Sparks asked.

"Yeah, he's goin'. Butch said he could."

"*Varooom, varooom, varooom,*" Gunner soared past them, making airplane noises. "He's here. I just seen him from the window. Hit it!"

Outside, Butch crouched in the shadow of the play-ground slide and waited for the lights to go out. Twenty minutes before, he had left Stanley with the jeep and insisted on going onto the grounds alone. He was pretty certain that Stanley was no better at sneaking around in the dark than he was at driving. Also, he was afraid that if Stanley got a look at some of the kids who would be coming with him, he might try to back out of the whole deal.

Butch checked the watch he had borrowed from Stanley. It was almost midnight. Once again, he felt the coil of rope he had brought from *Southwind,* and hoped that it had not gotten tangled up. Actually it was two ropes. The smaller one was called a "heaving line," and at one end of it was a large, heavy knot called a "monkey's fist," which made the line easy to throw. The other rope was heavy enough to climb down, and all along it, he had tied knots to make it easier to hold on to.

The orphanage was mostly dark. Except for the floodlights outside, only on the third floor were there still lights on in the boys' dormitory. Both the girls' floor and the ground floor where the matrons lived were dark and quiet.

Someone moved from behind the third-floor window. Seconds later, there was a flash from inside, and all the lights went out. *They did it,* Butch thought and ran toward the building.

"Butch? That you down there?" The voice sounded like Slug's.

"Yeah, of course it's me. I'm gonna throw ya a rope."

It took almost a dozen tries before the heaving line was finally through the window. Several more minutes passed before the heavier rope was pulled up and tied to the heater.

Gunner was the first boy down and, to Butch's surprise, he came quietly. "My engine quit," he whispered as he landed. Tadpole came down next, followed by Sparks.

23

"Okay, Slug," Butch called up in a loud whisper. "Let's go . . . you're next." A long silence followed. "Come on, we ain't got all night!"

"I can't, just can't," Slug called out in the darkness. "It's too far! I'll fall, I know I'll fall. An' then I'll splatter all over the playground like a big ol' bug, an' kids'll step on my guts and smear me all around and — "

"Shut up!"

"We gotta hurry," Sparks whispered. "The penguins'll get the lights back on any minute now."

It seemed to Butch as though there was only one thing to do. "You guys wait for us out by the main gate," he said. "I'll get Slug an' we'll meet ya there!" He spat on his hands, took a good grip on the rope, and started climbing up.

He was just passing the second floor when a window came open and the familiar voice of Maisy demanded, "Butch Hoover, what are you doing back here?"

"Be quiet!"

"You tell me what's going on or I'll start screaming," Maisy insisted.

"All right, some more of us guys are bustin' out. Now go back to bed, an' don't make no noise!" Butch whispered and kept climbing.

"You'll just get caught. You always do."

"Not if you keep yer big yap shut, we won't."

For a moment, Maisy pouted silently, and then said, "I want to go too."

"Like I told ya before, we ain't takin' no girls!"

Two seconds later, Maisy started screaming. The lights came on.

5

Butch reached for the third-floor window sill just as the floodlights blinded him.

"There's a boy climbing up the wall!" some girl was shouting.

"Come on, Slug, gimme a hand!" Butch called, but the window above remained empty. He cast a glance down over his shoulder and saw one of the matrons standing directly beneath him and shaking a stick. "I'm gonna get you, Slug!" he swore as he mustered the last of his failing strength and pulled himself in through the window.

Slug was sitting on his bed, with tears running down his face. "I'm sorry, Butch. I couldn't do it, I'm real scared of high places, I can't — "

Butch kicked him in the side. "Why, you yellow-belly — get up!" he yelled, but Slug just kept crying. "Get up, I said! We gotta get outa here!"

"Noooo!" Slug wailed. "I can't climb down no rope. I'll fall, I know I'll fall!"

Butch grabbed him by his collar and jerked him to his feet. "Then we'll do it another way," he cursed as he dragged him toward the door. There were six other boys still in the room. By now they were all laughing and calling Slug names.

"It's locked, it's always locked!" Slug moaned, pointing at the door. Just as he spoke, a key turned in the lock.

"It won't be for long!" Butch warned. The door opened just as both boys dove under one of the beds. Heavy footsteps thundered past as one of the matrons burst in and headed for the open window. "Now, go!" Butch whispered and crawled out between the beds. This time Slug needed no encouragement. He was up and running in an instant. They ran through the open door together, and Butch stopped only long enough to slam it shut and lock it behind them. "That ought to slow 'em down a little," he said, tossing the key down the stairs.

They reached the second-floor landing, flew past the door to the girls' room, and then stopped short. Matron Grabouski was blocking their path, smiling. In one hand she held the key Butch had just thrown.

"I didn't want ta do it!" Slug screamed. "I like it here, I really do. I don't care if the food's no good and there's rats and no heat, and — !"

The door beside them opened suddenly, and Maisy pulled on Slug's arm. "In here!" she hissed. Butch pushed from the other side and, in a moment, they were in the girls' dormitory, with the door closed behind them. "Quick," Maisy said, "go out the window, your rope's right beside it!" Just then, twenty-four girls began screaming and throwing pillows.

"It's no good!" Butch insisted as he ducked a pillow that hit Slug right in the face. "Slug won't go!"

Matron Grabouski was beating on the door as Maisy pushed them toward the window. "Yeah? Well, he better, because if he stays in here, these girls are going to kill him!"

"I'll go, I'll go!" Slug was yelling. "Anything's better'n being beat ta death with pillows!" With both Butch and Maisy pushing on him, Slug finally climbed out the window. As soon as he was on the ground, Butch followed him out. On the window ledge, he hesitated for a moment.

"Thanks, Maisy," he said. "Sorry ya can't come with us."

"So don't worry about it, okay?" Maisy shrugged, with a silly smile on her face. Just then, the door came off its hinges. Matron Grabouski stomped in, carrying a sledge hammer.

Butch slid down the rope and hit the ground hard. He rolled over and got to his feet running. Ahead, he could hear Slug panting as they ran for the gate.

It took quite a while to work their way to the road. Since several of the matrons were out searching the grounds, much of the time was spent crawling through bushes and keeping to the shadows. It took even longer to find the rest of the boys and get them to the waiting jeep.

"Come on, hurry up," Stanley called as they began climbing in. "You guys certainly took long enough."

"Oh, yeah?" It was Slug who spoke. "You ain't had no six-foot-tall matrons chasin' you, so shut yer trap an' drive."

"Cool off," Butch told them. As the jeep lurched out onto the road, he looked in the tiny back seat and thought he counted five heads. "Okay, did everybody make it?"

"Yeah," Gunner answered. "We all made it, but we got Cockroach too."

There was a general round of moans and boos. "Hey!" Cockroach said sharply. "You guys are gonna need me. You just wait."

"There's another problem," Tadpole piped up from his wedged-in position between the seats. "One of us is a girl!"

Butch peered over the seat. "Maisy? Where do ya think you're goin'?"

"As far away from the penguins as I can."

"Not with us, you ain't," Slug chimed in and tried to push her out of the jeep.

Her small fist landed on Slug's nose. "Oh yeah, fatso? Why not?"

" 'Cause there ain't no girls allowed, that's why!" Butch argued.

"You call that a reason?"

"Girls are dumb, and they smell funny," Sparks laughed.

"We smell funny because we take baths. 'Course, you wouldn't know about baths, since you've never had one."

Slug laughed. "I take one of them every spring, whether or not I need it."

"Will you idiots all shut up?" Stanley yelled at the top of his lungs.

For a moment, there was complete silence. Then Tadpole asked, "Who's he?"

"Yeah," Cockroach added, "and who died and left him boss?"

Stanley steered the jeep around a corner and almost ran into the ditch. "I'm Stanley Merriweather and — "

"Stanley? So what is a Stanley?" Cockroach asked, peering over the seat. "Is it an animal? A bird? No, I think it is a jerk."

"Whatever it is," Maisy added, "it is not a driver."

Slug grabbed at Stanley's tie and pulled until it almost choked him. "Hey, guys, look at this! He's got a tie, and cute little bitty short pants."

"A rich kid — let's roll 'im."

"I never seen nothin' like him before," Slug said, burping in Stanley's face.

Butch put a hand on Slug's nose and shoved him back into the seat. "Cut it out! Ya want ta kill us all? He's a jerk, but he's tryin' to drive, remember?"

All at once Stanley slammed on the brakes and the

jeep slid to a halt in the light of a street lamp. "All right," he said through gritted teeth. "That's it. Everybody out! Hoover, you said you could get a crew. This is no crew; this is a bunch of monkeys. I'm not taking them back to my grandfather's yacht."

"So who cares?" Maisy challenged. "We don't want to see your old yacht anyway — whatever that is."

"Yeah, what's a yacht?" Tadpole asked.

"Hold it, hold it, hold it!" Butch cut in and waited until everyone was quiet. "Okay, I'm gonna tell all of ya what the deal is. If you like it, fine. If ya don't, then you're on your own and no hard feelings." He paused and looked around the young faces crowded into the jeep. "Deal?"

There was a general nodding of heads, and Butch spent the next several minutes trying to explain what was going on.

"I'm with you," Sparks said when he had finished. "But do we gotta take him with us?" He pointed at Stanley.

"Yeah, Sparks, we gotta take him too."

"I'm in," Tadpole and Gunner answered in unison.

"Me too, Butch, I got nowhere real important ta go," Slug said, and then laughed.

Cockroach shrugged. "Like I said, you guys are gonna need me."

Butch turned to Maisy. "So, what about you?"

"She can't come," Slug insisted.

"I don't know about her. You did not say anything about a girl — " Stanley started to say.

Butch cut him off. "I changed my mind," he said. "I say she can come. If she hadn't helped me and Slug, the penguins would've got us for sure. We owe her."

"I'm coming, and you jerks ain't big enough to stop me," Maisy insisted.

Reluctantly, Stanley threw up his hands. "All right, all right, she may come along. Now, can we all please get going?"

6

The rain had stopped and skies were clearing when Captain Merriweather arrived aboard the *Southwind* early the next morning. He found Stanley on deck, sitting dejectedly by the wheel and drinking a cup of hot chocolate.

"Good morning, Stanley," Merriweather said in a rather disappointed voice as he sat down on one of the winches. "The squadron commander wants us to sail very soon. I don't suppose we have a crew, do we?"

"Actually, Grandfather, I'm not certain just what we have, but I believe, counting Hoover, there are six of them."

"Six?" Merriweather immediately perked up. "Well, that should do nicely."

Stanley shook his head. "You really should see them before you make up your mind. Except for Hoover, I don't think they have any experience."

Merriweather huffed. "No matter," he said, getting up. "I can buy us a couple of days to get squared away, and then we'll have a couple of more days sailing time to reach our patrol area. That should be plenty of time to shake them down and get them settled in." As he talked, Merriweather walked briskly to the main hatchway and descended the stairs into the salon. The first thing he saw was Slug, sleeping on top of the table.

"What is that? And why is it sleeping on the table?" Merriweather asked.

"The others call him 'Slug'," Stanley answered sadly. "And that is where he passed out. It was a couple of hours ago. He went pretty crazy for a while after he got into the galley and ate a whole pound of sugar."

"Astounding," Merriweather commented, mostly to himself, and turned his attention toward the radio room located just aft of the salon. Someone there was whistling.

"They call that one 'Sparks'," Stanley explained. "He found those boxes of electronic equipment the navy brought yesterday. He's been in there ever since. I have no idea what he is doing."

"Vacuum tubes," Sparks said without looking up from the navy manual he was reading. "I've found two bad ones already. Get me a USN35289-A512 out of that box over there."

Absently, Merriweather began fumbling around in a box full of tubes.

"I've calibrated the radios," Sparks announced, "and got a commo check from some ship that said I wasn't supposed to be talking on that frequency."

Stanley groaned.

"No sweat," Sparks continued. "I told him this was the aircraft carrier *Lexington*."

"Interesting," Merriweather noted as he handed Sparks a tube. "How are you coming with that listening device?"

"It's called a 'magnetometer', and it's not actually a listening device." Sparks picked up a screwdriver and disappeared under the chart table. "It reads variations in the earth's natural magnetic field caused by any large concentration of ferrous metal, such as the steel hull of a submarine. It's really very simple."

"How soon will you have it working?"

Sparks crawled out from under the chart table. "Seems to check out okay, but I can't really test it until we get away from all these other ships." He exchanged his screwdriver for a pair of wire cutters and disappeared again.

Merriweather stared thoughtfully at the mess of scattered parts and boxes. "Carry on, Mr. Sparks," he said at length and left.

"He's just small for his age," Stanley said as they started forward.

In the galley, they found Tadpole, eating a bowl of Wheaties. "Well, good morning son," Merriweather said. "How old are you? No, don't tell me, you're small for your age."

Tadpole shrugged and slurped milk out of his bowl. "I don't know. Nobody ever told me. Butch might know. We could ask him."

"I will ask him," Merriweather said, and continued forward, where he bumped into Cockroach coming out of one of the cabins.

"Hey, good morning there. You must be the captain, uh, Merriworth or something like that?" Cockroach rattled off.

"Merriweather," the captain returned. "And how old are you?"

"Thirty-five," Cockroach answered without a second's hesitation. "I'm a midget."

"*Varooom, varoom, varoom!*" Gunner made airplane sounds as he swooped out of the crew quarters and past them into the galley.

Merriweather watched him go, then turned to Stanley and raised one eyebrow.

Stanley grinned. "He thinks he's an airplane."

"Humph. I'll have a word with you on deck," Merriweather said and pointed toward the hatchway. "Immediately."

As they stepped out on deck, Maisy brushed past them dressed in an oversized pair of dungarees and a denim shirt that came almost to her knees. She was humming a Glenn Miller tune and snapping her fingers as she disappeared down the hatch.

Merriweather took a deep breath and held it until it seemed he might explode at any moment. Then he released it and nudged Stanley out on deck. "What have you done?" he demanded.

Stanley took a couple of steps backward and suddenly spotted Butch walking down the pier with his hands in his pockets. "Uh, well, it wasn't me, Grandfather . . . it was Hoover. It was all his fault!"

Merriweather turned quickly to Butch as he stepped aboard, and repeated his question.

Butch nodded; it was time for the truth. "You're right, it's my fault, and it was all a real bad idea." For the next twenty minutes, Butch tried to explain what he had done and who the strange assortment of kids were who now infested *Southwind*.

"I shouldn't have got 'em into this," he concluded sadly. "But after I couldn't get into the navy or the army or the Marines Corps or anything else — and then, when you needed a crew so bad, well, like I said, it was a bad idea."

Merriweather nodded thoughtfully. "What orphanage did you say you were from?"

"Greystone."

"That's not an orphanage — that's one small step from the state penitentiary!"

Butch nodded. "Yeah, we all been in the clink for something."

Merriweather lit his pipe and puffed thoughtfully on

it for a while. "And you," he pointed at Butch. "What did you get in trouble for?"

"Stole a boat."

Merriweather looked suddenly interested. "Really?" he said.

"Yeah. When my dad died, bankers come and took our skipjack." He looked away. "I stole it back, but they caught me."

Merriweather only nodded.

"So, ya see, these guys ain't got nothin' to lose," Butch continued. "They got no parents, they got no kin, they got no nothin'. I figured they'd be better off here, than back at Greystone."

Merriweather rose and walked slowly to *Southwind*'s wide stern. For a long time he stood staring up at her masts. It seemed to Butch that he must be remembering how her sails looked when the wind was in them and the sea was running her rail under. Or perhaps he was remembering other ships and other voyages from long ago.

Finally, he returned and stood very straight as he faced Stanley. "Mr. Merriweather," the old commodore said, with a new twinkle in his eyes, "you will be first mate. Mr. Hoover will be our number two." He reached into his pocket and removed a gold pocket watch, opened it, and then felt the wind on his face. "I am off to see the squadron commander and try to convince him I need a few more days to train the new crew. Until I return, you two are in charge. Now hop to it, and let's get this ship ready for sea," he said and walked briskly ashore.

7

By early afternoon, *Southwind*'s decks were beginning to look as if they had already been through a war — and lost. "We have got to get organized," Stanley sighed as he surveyed the mess of supplies and equipment. "Somewhere, we are supposed to have another three hundred feet of line for the sea anchors. Then there are all those radio parts and wires that Sparks says he has to have in order to hook up the radio direction finder. We still don't have hardly any medical supplies."

Butch finished lashing down one of the two new life rafts, which had been delivered that morning. "How is Maisy doing in the galley?" he asked.

Stanley shrugged. "I can't tell. Are you sure she knows anything about cooking?"

"Nope, but she's a girl. Aren't girls sort of born knowing about stuff like that?"

Stanley shrugged and then looked at the clipboard he had been carrying all day. "There are still an awful lot of things we've got to get somewhere."

35

As they talked, Cockroach strolled up, eating a biscuit. For a while he stared over Stanley's shoulder. "Told ya, you guys were going to need me," he said between bites. "Gimme the list."

"Why?" Stanley demanded, clutching his clipboard.

"Better give him the list," Butch insisted. "If there's one thing Cockroach can do, it's swipe stuff."

Stanley looked shocked. "You mean he can *steal* all this?"

"Hey, punk!" Cockroach snapped, pushing Stanley against the main mast and taking the clipboard. "Watch your mouth. This is the navy, right? Well, here they call it 'requisition'." Quickly, he scanned the list. "Okay, so normally I work alone. But there's a bunch of specialized stuff here, so I'm takin' Sparks. And Butch, you come too, so's you can pick out just what you want."

Fifteen minutes later Cockroach led the way as Butch and Sparks followed him toward several large wooden buildings marked "Quartermaster Supply" on Pier 7. Cockroach whistled as he walked along with his hands in his pockets and his cap pulled down low over his eyes.

"Okay," he announced as he raised one hand and stopped. "First thing is to get us some duds."

"Duds? What for?" Sparks asked.

"Sailor clothes, ya dummy," Cockroach replied. "Ya know, those stupid-looking little white hats, and coats maybe, the blue ones." He pointed at a sign which read "Head." "Wait around the corner. I'm goin' in there."

"What's that?" Sparks asked.

"That's what the navy calls a restroom," Butch said.

Cockroach disappeared inside, and a couple of minutes later, he came out running with his arms loaded with coats. One sailor hat was on his head, and two more were sticking out of his pockets. "Quick," he said. "Put these on."

The supply warehouse was bustling with men, loading and unloading all sorts of supplies. No one paid much attention to three short sailors with a clipboard and a list who began loading a four-wheeled cart with coils of rope, boxes of food, and medical supplies.

They left with Cockroach still leading the way and whistling. Two doors down, he stopped in front of a sign which read "Radio Repair Shop." Here Cockroach changed his tactics. He pulled off his sailor's coat and hat, felt around in his pocket, and took out a fancy-looking watch. "Use the back door, Sparks, I'll keep the clerk busy while you get what you need."

With that, Cockroach walked through the front door and up to the counter, where a sailor was writing something on a form. "Hey, chief," Cockroach began, "need a watch?"

After five minutes of bargaining, the sailor owned a new watch and Cockroach was walking out the door, counting his money. Around the corner, he met Sparks and Butch. Each of them was holding a big box full of electronic equipment.

"So, ya get what you need?" Cockroach asked as he pocketed his money.

"Yeah, I got all kinds of stuff here," Sparks said, and then noticed the money Cockroach had. "Wow. You sold your watch, just so we could get this stuff?"

"Yeah, ain't I a saint?" Cockroach smiled as he pulled two more watches out of his pocket, chose one, and strapped it on his wrist. "Now, let's scoot, before his quits workin'."

When they returned to *Southwind,* a truck was just leaving, and several heavy, wooden crates were stacked on deck. Stanley was looking at a paper and Gunner was prying open one of the crates with a crowbar. "We better get this stuff outa sight," Butch said, pointing at the cart, "before someone sees it."

Sparks carried his two boxes below and then disappeared into the radio room, humming a tune and totally happy. By the time the cart had been emptied, Gunner had one of the crates open and was holding up a rifle. *"Pow, pow, pow!"* he shouted as he ran around the deck, pointing the rifle in all directions.

"Gimme that!" Butch shouted at him and grabbed the rifle as Gunner ran past. "What d'ya think you're doin'? This ain't no game of cowboys and Indians."

"We must lock these up in the captain's cabin," Stanley insisted. "Now, what else is in there?"

"I dunno," Gunner said and picked up an egg-shaped thing with a pin and a handle on one side. "Looks kinda like a little metal pineapple. Don't let Slug see it. He'll probably eat it." Gunner started pulling on the pin, trying to remove it. "I wonder what this is for?" he said.

"Don't touch that!" Stanley screamed in his face. "That's a hand grenade, a bomb, you idiot! If you take the pin out, it blows up!"

Gunner looked thoughtfully at the grenade. "Oh yeah? I'll remember that," he said and tossed it to Stanley, who almost dropped it three times before he handed it to Butch.

"Lock these up too," Stanley said through gritted teeth.

"We gonna shoot Germans?" Tadpole asked as he walked up and looked in the box.

"Will if we see one, I guess," Butch answered.

"If we see them?" Stanley said. "We will be lucky if we even hear them with our electronic gear."

"Varoom, varoom! Bomber number one cleared for take off," Gunner said and ran below with his arms full of grenades.

Cockroach had picked up one of the rifles and was looking closely at it. "This thing was made in 1917," he announced. "What do they give us this junk for?"

Stanley shrugged. "We won't need it anyway."

"Three lousy old rifles and some hand grenades? I think we need something better than this."

Stanley said, "These will do fine. Now help me carry them down below."

"No way," Cockroach insisted. "We need some real guns." And without further comment, he walked off, onto the dock.

"Stop him!" Stanley ordered, turning to Butch.

Butch shook his head and started below with a box of grenades. "Let him go. He'll be back — maybe," he said.

Cockroach passed Merriweather just as he stepped onto the gangplank. Merriweather turned and looked after him, but Cockroach just kept walking. "Where is he off to?" the captain asked.

"Probably gone for good," Stanley answered.

Merriweather then looked around at the mess on *Southwind*'s deck. "How are we doing?" he asked cautiously.

"Not too well," Stanley admitted as he followed Merriweather below, where the mess was even worse.

When they passed Maisy, Merriweather asked how she was doing in the galley.

"I dunno," Maisy shrugged. "I've been working in the kitchen all day."

Again Merriweather huffed. "Well, that's nice. What are you serving for the evening meal?"

Maisy stared up at him for a long time. "You mean you expect me to cook something?" she asked with a frightened look in her eyes.

"Yeah, Maisy," Butch cut in. "You said you could handle it. That's why we gave you the job."

Maisy frowned until her eyes crossed. "Anybody like peanut butter?" she asked.

"That will be fine, Maisy," Merriweather said and walked to the radio room. Inside, nothing appeared to have changed much since morning. Sparks had a technical manual in one hand, and his head inside one of the radios. "Mr. Sparks," Merriweather said. "Can you turn on the radio and get us a weather report?"

Sparks looked up, thought for a moment, and said, "Not right now, but maybe in about ten minutes — that is, if nothing else catches fire."

Merriweather turned away and sighed deeply. "Stanley," he said, "I think we should have a meeting of all the crew. Would you get everyone together in the salon, please?"

In a matter of minutes *Southwind*'s salon was crowded with young faces. Butch counted heads and then turned to Merriweather. "Everybody's here except Cockroach. We don't know if he's even coming back."

"Thank you," Merriweather said rather sadly. For a moment, he let his eyes wander over the odd collection of young people. "First, I want to tell all of you exactly what has happened. I have been asked to take *Southwind* to sea immediately. There is some bad weather offshore, and one of the other armed yachts has been forced to come in. Of course, I cannot do that."

Merriweather paused and again looked around the room. "I believe that, if I had more time — a couple of weeks, perhaps — I might make a crew out of you. But now I can see there is just too much for you to learn, in order for us to sail anytime in the near future."

"We ain't got much time," Butch interrupted. "We're all on the run."

Merriweather nodded sadly. "Yes, I know that, and so I must inform the squadron commander that *Southwind* does not have a crew."

"We ain't goin' back to that orphanage," Slug insisted, and pounded his fist on the table. "Not never."

Butch tried desperately to think of some solution. "Excuse me, Captain Merriweather," he said. "But could we all have a few minutes alone?"

"Certainly," Merriweather nodded. "I'll be in my cabin. Come along, Stanley."

"I'll stay."

"No, ya won't," Slug challenged and threw a biscuit

at him. "You ain't one of us." With that, Stanley followed Merriweather out of the salon.

"Okay, I say we steal that jeep again and make a run for it," Slug proposed loudly.

"Yeah, right!" It was Cockroach who answered him, suddenly dropping down through one of the forward hatches. "That'd be real smart. Where we gonna go, Slug? You thought of that?"

"We could go to Alaska," Gunner suggested. "And find gold."

"You couldn't find gold, and you couldn't find Alaska if you had a road map printed on your face."

Tadpole was sitting on the floor under the table. "I wanna go kill Germans," he said.

"You don't know nothin' about killing nobody, ya little shrimp," Maisy said, kicking at him.

Cockroach sauntered across the salon, with a toothpick hanging on his lip, and leaned against the hatchway. "I say the little kid's right. We got no place to go but out there." He jerked his thumb in the direction of the ocean. "We're all a bunch of losers. We ain't worth nothin', and we never been worth nothin'. Then, all of a sudden, Lady Luck comes waltzin' along and gives us one chance, one lousy chance ta do somethin' important, and right off the bat, we blow it."

"We don't know nothin' about boats and stuff," Slug whined and stood up.

Cockroach crossed the salon and stuck his nose in Slug's face. "Yeah, that's right. You don't know nothin' about nothin'. So what did you do today ta start learning something about boats and stuff? You ate sugar 'til ya passed out, and then laid around puking your guts."

Slug sat down frowning, sniffed loudly, and folded his arms.

Cockroach stared the rest of them down. "Now, we got two guys, Butch and Stanley there, who know somethin' about this sailin' stuff. So the way I figure it, if the rest of ya got anything but dirty wax between your ears, you'll do what they say — get this boat put together and ready to go. Then you'll go in there to Captain Merriweather and beg him to take us all outa here, fast." He paused, and then added, "So, that's all I gotta say."

There followed a long, nervous silence. "We'll probably all starve 'cause we ain't got no cook," Slug whined.

Maisy stood up and started for the galley, without a word.

"I'll help, I know how to cook," Tadpole called and followed her. Seconds later, Sparks headed for the radio room.

Cockroach turned to Butch, who had remained silent during most of the meeting. "Okay, so they're motivated. I got a couple of things in a cart outside I gotta get hid. Then what do you want us to do?"

Butch thought for a moment before he said, "Let's get everything tied down on deck, then we'll pull the sail covers off." Cockroach nodded and started past him. "Hey," Butch added, "thanks."

8

Gray seas rolled beneath *Southwind*'s keel, and scudding spray blew across her decks. Her wind-filled sails stood wet and dripping as the schooner fought her way farther and farther out into the Atlantic Ocean. Butch put his weight against the wheel, forcing the ship to hold her course as he felt the forces of wind and sea which drove her crashing through the waves.

"You're getting the feel of her now, lad," Merriweather said from beside him. "Don't steer her too much. When *Southwind* is trimmed right, she will nearly sail herself."

All things considered, Butch felt happy to be at sea once again. He could not even remember how many years had passed since he steered his father's skipjack, homeward bound with the decks piled high with oysters, but the memories remained clear and precious.

Learning to steer *Southwind* had been easy. She was big — a hundred feet long and weighing almost a hundred tons — and she handled differently than the skipjack. But the thrill of feeling her surge beneath him, the force at which she crashed headlong into towering waves, was the most exciting thing Butch had ever experienced. He quickly came to love the frequent two-hour watches he spent at her wheel. Somehow, being cold and wet and hungry did not seem quite as bad here as it had on land.

They had been at sea for almost three days now. He doubted that any one of the crew had slept since the morning after they first arrived aboard. Slug and Gunner were still too seasick to even begin learning anything. Cockroach was a soupy shade of green, but he still managed to help out. At the moment, he had the bow watch. Sparks was sick too, but he was somehow standing his watches in the radio room. Maisy and Tadpole remained totally unaffected by seasickness. The night before, they had actually managed to cook some sort of soup which most everyone drank without vomiting.

Stanley was probably in the best shape of anyone. He, of course, had sailed on *Southwind* before and, along with Butch and Captain Merriweather, was working almost without rest.

"Another day, my lad," Merriweather called above the wind, as if he had read Butch's thoughts. "Then the weather should ease a bit by the time we reach our patrol area."

"Yes, sir," Butch agreed. It seemed to him that it was almost a miracle that a half-dozen screwball orphans had actually gotten *Southwind* ready for sea and convinced Captain Merriweather to take them. Back at Greystone, they had all been loners, looking out for only themselves and never working together at anything. Out here, maybe it would be different.

"Do you think there'll be many German submarines out in the area we're goin' to?" Butch asked.

"Hard to say," the captain answered as green water surged across the deck, and he held on to a shroud. "We'll be off the main shipping lanes by a little bit, and so far there's been no activity reported there. It will most likely be a very quiet patrol."

The German submarine U-132 was a ship designed and built for only one purpose — the killing of other ships. Her hull was 220 feet of cold steel, sleek, and as streamlined as the schools of fish that fled before her. Like the sharks, she too was a hunter, built to stalk beneath the surface, to kill from silent ambush, and then slink away into the night, to kill again.

Her captain was Jorchen Meyer, a blond man with a blond beard and bloodshot eyes. He stood in the conning tower, bathed in the eerie red glow of the U-boat's night lights, and watched the needle on a depth gauge as the U-boat inched its way closer and closer to the surface.

"Up periscope," he ordered. Somewhere, a handle was pulled, hydraulic oil hissed, and the periscope rose. He pressed his eyes against the lenses and he could see the ocean's surface thirty feet above him. He turned the scope in a full circle, scanning the horizon quickly for any sign of ship or aircraft. Suddenly, he stopped short. *"Mein Gott,"* he whispered as he adjusted the periscope's focus. A smile spread slowly across his face. "A schooner," he said aloud. "I would not have expected to find one out here."

In the last war, she would have been worth sinking, he mused. Years ago, during the First World War, sailing ships had been favorite targets for submarines. They had only to surface, fire a shot across the bow, and then give the crew time to get to their lifeboats. A few high-explosive rounds i˙ ⁺ɴ the hull, and the schooner would be nothing but match sticks, scattered on the sea. But that was another war, he reminded himself. This was a much dirtier war, especially when the mission included landing a spy on the American coast.

Meyer returned his thoughts to the schooner as it sailed in the crosshairs of his periscope. This little one was too small to carry cargo. *She must be a yacht,* he thought, and then he noticed that she was painted navy gray and carried a white number on her bow. He laughed out loud. "What is this? She thinks she is a warship." Stepping away, and pointing at the periscope, he spoke to the lieutenant beside him. "What do you make of that, Schultz?"

"Some sort of makeshift patrol vessel, perhaps," Schultz guessed as he looked through the scope. "I count three antennas on her masts — too many radios for an ordinary sailing ship. Shall we surface and sink her with the deck gun, sir?"

Something inside him was saying that the tiny little schooner could somehow be trouble. He could follow her until dark, work his way around in front of her, and surface. Then a couple of quick shots and it would all be over.

He had almost made up his mind to do it when Schultz was handed a piece of paper. "Sonar reports a contact, sir. Slow speed screws to the south . . . sounds like a freighter."

"Lay a course for it," Meyer snapped, suddenly changing his mind. "We go for the big fish."

Darkness had fallen when Captain Merriweather finally left Butch at the wheel and went below. He stopped in the radio room and found Sparks twisting knobs on one of the radios.

"Anything interesting?" Merriweather asked.

Sparks pulled off his earphones. "Everything is real quiet. I haven't heard nothing in a couple of hours."

"How about that magnetometer?" Merriweather's voice sounded very tired. "Do you think it's working?"

Sparks frowned at the black box with two meters on

it. "I'm not sure. I thought I picked up something on it about an hour ago, but then it went away."

Merriweather nodded. "Well, keep at it, lad. I'm going to try to get a little rest. Been feeling awfully tired lately," he said, starting to leave.

Sparks put the earphones back on his head. "Wait, wait!" he called excitedly, just as Merriweather was stepping out of the radio room. "I got something on the radio. Here . . . listen. I'll switch it over to the speaker."

He threw a switch and static crackled over the speaker. A faint voice called, "SOS! SOS! Steamship *Orion*. Attacked by submarine, ninety miles north-northwest of Great Isaac's Light."

Merriweather was already at the chart table, marking a tiny gray "X" where the freighter reported to be. "She's very close," he said quietly. "We can try to relay the message, but I think it's going to be up to us to try to reach her." He cast a worried frown at Sparks.

"I was hoping nothing like this would happen for a while," he said.

47

9

A couple of hours after dark, the wind dropped and the sea smoothed out to long rolling swells. There had been no other messages over the radio during the hours that slipped by as *Southwind* sailed steadily on, toward the freighter's last known position. Stanley had taken over the wheel, and Merriweather stood beside him. Their faces glowed in the dim compass light.

"What are we to do if we find her?" Stanley asked.

"We don't even know if she was hit. She may have been lucky and slipped away in the darkness. But if she was torpedoed, then we shall do whatever we can," Merriweather answered tiredly. "Look for survivors is probably about all."

" 'Spose she's still afloat?" Butch asked. "What do we do then?"

"Well, it's a bit dangerous to report a damaged ship over the radio. The navy is afraid that other U-boats might be listening in and then they'd come like a pack of sharks to finish her off. So about all we can do is stand by and give her whatever assistance her captain asks for."

Stanley sighed. "As slow as we are tonight, I'm certain it will be all over long before we get there."

Merriweather groaned and looked at the sails. "Mr. Hoover," he ordered, "you'd better take these binoculars and go aloft. Keep a sharp eye out. That ship cannot be far away now."

Butch hung the binoculars around his neck. "Yes, sir," he answered, and scurried up the mainmast ratlines. Two-thirds of the way up the mast was a little platform which Merriweather called the "crow's nest." Around it was a metal railing, and there was just enough space for one man to stand. The view was breathtaking, Butch thought as he settled himself against the rail and looked out over the endless expanse of ocean. Scattered clouds were scudding across the eastern sky. Behind them, the moon played hide-and-seek, casting pale, ghostly pools of light among the waves. It was all so peaceful that it did not seem possible there was a war going on.

When Butch finally spotted the freighter, it was only a couple of miles away. At first it appeared as just a streak of dark shadow against the clouds, but suddenly the clouds parted and, for a few moments, moonlight silhouetted the dark ship.

"Captain Merriweather!" Butch called. "I see her!"

"Where away?"

"Off the starboard bow, about two miles." Butch refocused his glasses on the ship. "She's got no lights on, and she don't look like she's movin'. Her stern is ridin' up kinda high. I think maybe she's sinking."

"Any sign of her lifeboats?" Merriweather called nervously.

"Ain't seen 'em yet."

The dark, seemingly lifeless ship grew steadily larger as *Southwind* approached. Butch trained his glasses on the wheelhouse, scanning the dark windows for any sign of life.

"What do you make of it, Grandfather?" Stanley asked in barely a whisper as *Southwind* luft her sails and pointed her bow into the wind. Slowly, they drifted into the shadow of the freighter's hull.

"She seems to be abandoned," Merriweather answered. "Perhaps a U-boat hit her once and assumed she would sink. The crew may have taken to the lifeboats, and are out of sight by now, I suppose."

Just then, Butch called down from the crow's nest. "I'm not sure, but I think I just saw somebody moving around on her."

Merriweather rubbed his chin and cast a worried glance around the deck. "I must go aboard her," he said at last.

"Board her?" Stanley objected. "Why, wouldn't that be awfully dangerous? I mean, she does look like she's about to sink."

"If there is someone aboard, they might be injured, or perhaps they've lost their lifeboats," Merriweather insisted. "Besides that, we are supposed to make certain that her charts and code books are not left aboard." Before Stanley could object further, Merriweather called for Butch to come down from the crow's nest. In only a couple of minutes, they had turned out the crew and lowered *Southwind*'s little tender into the water.

"I should go," Stanley insisted. "I'm first mate."

"No," Merriweather corrected him sharply. "I must leave you in charge of *Southwind*. You are the only one aboard who I am certain can sail her home if something goes wrong. I shall take Mr. Hoover with me, and a couple of others to help row."

"I wanna go," Slug announced. "I'm startin' ta feel a lot better now."

"Count me in too," Cockroach added.

"Very well," Merriweather said with a frown. "Then let us get moving."

The little tender pulled unsteadily toward the darkened freighter until the wet steel hull towered above them, blocking out the sky. Butch and Cockroach rowed while Merriweather steered and Slug sat in the bow. Occasional waves broke across the tender's low sides and slapped their faces with cool spray.

"Can you see any way to get up the side?" Merriweather called as they neared the ship.

"Yeah, yeah, there's a kind of a ladder, over this way some more. It looks kind of high, but there's a rope hanging from it," Slug answered and tried to grab the dangling line. On the third try he made it.

"Very good," Merriweather said and made his way forward. "Oh, my," he said as he saw how far the ladder was above the boat. "That's a long way up. I don't think I can make it."

"Butch can make it," Slug suggested. "He's real good at climbing ropes."

"Well, I don't . . ." Merriweather started to object, but Butch was already climbing up the rope.

"I wanna go!" Slug said.

"You'll never climb that," Cockroach replied. "Now get outa my way."

"No!" Slug wailed. "I wanna go, I wanna go! I don't wanna sit here in no little old boat!"

"Shut up!" Butch whispered loudly. "Here, give me your hand. Cockroach, now you give him a shove." With considerable grunting and groaning, they managed to lift Slug high enough for him to grab the dangling ladder. "Come on," Butch told him and started climbing the ladder. Behind them, Cockroach picked up two flashlights and followed them up.

"Be careful, lads," Merriweather called after them.

Butch reached the freighter's railing and pulled himself onto the deck. Chills ran up his spine as he looked

53

around the deserted ship and listened to its creaking and groaning. Before him were the forward cargo hatches. Somewhere a pulley was loose and banging against a mast. High above were the darkened windows of the wheelhouse, where he thought he had seen movement earlier. Now there was only darkness.

Slug was panting when he climbed over the rail and joined him on the deck. Seconds later, Cockroach also reached the deck. For a few moments the three boys stared silently at the ship. Then Slug whispered, "Hey, this is a scary place. I mean, a really scary place."

"Yeah, Slug," Cockroach said. "Real scary. So, let's get moving. Merriweather said we should get the code books. So, what are the code books and where do we find 'em?"

"They'd be in the captain's safe, if he didn't take 'em with him," Butch answered as they entered a doorway and found themselves inside the ship. Iron stairs led up from the end of a short passage. "This way, maybe," Butch said.

The stairs ended at the deserted wheelhouse. Inside, they flashed their lights on the chart table. "No charts," Butch said. "That's good. The captain probably took them when he left."

"Yeah," Slug whispered, "but what I wanna know is, where did he go?"

Behind the wheelhouse, they found the captain's cabin. "Holy cow," Slug whispered as they entered. "This guy's messier than me." The mattress had been pulled from the bunk and ripped apart. The drawers of a small, metal desk had been emptied onto the floor, and clothes lay scattered everywhere.

"He ain't messy, ya dope," Cockroach said. "Somebody ransacked the joint."

"There's the safe, or what's left of it," Butch said as his flashlight beam fell on a small opening in the wall.

On the floor in front of it lay a round door with broken hinges.

Cockroach knelt down and examined it closely. "Somebody blew it open," he observed. "And that ain't good, since I figure the captain would not need to crack his own safe."

"Huh?" Slug asked as he picked his way to a porthole by the bunk.

"Germans?" Butch breathed.

"Hey, Butch — " Slug said, his voice sounding muffled with his head outside the porthole.

"Shut up. We're tryin' ta think!" Butch cut him off. "Yeah, Germans. It could be," he said to Cockroach.

"And you said you saw somebody moving around up here."

"Hey, Butch, you ever see one of them German submarines?" Slug asked again.

"No, I never seen one. Now, be quiet."

Cockroach looked nervously around him and whispered, "They might still be aboard."

"I think I know what they look like," Slug said.

"What looks like?" Butch snapped.

"One of them submarines. It's long and black and it kind of glides through the water like a shark, and there's this big gun on the front of it."

"Yeah, Slug, that's what a submarine looks like."

Slug pulled his head back inside the porthole and looked sick. "I was afraid you were gonna say that," he cried.

"Why, what are — "

Slug pointed out the porthole. "Because there's one of 'em right out there beside this ship!" he whispered.

10

The moon had once again pushed between the clouds and, in its pale glow, they saw the U-boat gliding in silently toward the freighter. Butch realized that, since *Southwind* had approached from the other side, they had not seen it before. Likewise, the U-boat, he hoped, had not seen *Southwind*.

"Let's scram," Cockroach said, already headed for the door. But before he got there, voices echoed in the hallway. They were not speaking English.

"Oooh nooo!" Slug wailed. "They're right outside. Now we're all gonna die."

"Shut yer trap," Butch threatened him, "or I'll knock yer block off."

Heavy footsteps sounded down the hall and the yellowish beam of a flashlight played on the wall. Slug had stuck four fingers in his mouth trying to keep himself quiet. Now he was making funny, gurgling sounds.

"Hide, quick!" Cockroach hissed, and all three boys dove for cover. Slug burrowed like a mole under the torn mattress, Cockroach ducked behind the desk, and Butch shrunk into a corner behind an overturned filing cabinet. They listened as several men hurried past the cabin and took the stairs back down to the deck.

Butch peeked down the hall. "Okay," he whispered, "they've gone."

Cockroach moved beside him. "Wonder what they was doin' here?" he asked.

"Same thing we were, I guess," Butch replied. "What else?"

"I don't know, but we better get outa here. Hey Slug, come on!"

Slug crawled out from under the mattress, with his fingers still in his mouth. Only now, his face was starting to turn blue. "Get yer fist outa yer mouth, ya dummy!" Butch told him, grabbing his arm. "Ya wanta suffocate yerself?"

Instead of following the Germans, the boys ran down the hallway in the other direction and took a different set of stairs back to deck level.

"Hey, look," Slug whispered as he shined his light into the galley, where plates of food still sat on several tables. "They all left so fast, they never finished eating."

"You smell somethin' burning?" Butch asked.

"Probably food, on the stove," Slug suggested and walked into the galley. "Oh, wow!" he exclaimed suddenly. "Cherry pies, big ol' juicy red cherry pies!"

Cockroach ignored him and sniffed the air. "Yeah, I smell it, and it ain't comin' from no kitchen." He pointed to a ladder which led down into one of the cargo holds. "You ever smell dynamite fuse?" he asked.

Butch shook his head. "No, I never — "

"Ya have now," Cockroach said, "and we gotta get outa here fast!"

"Slug!" Butch called. "Quit stuffin' yer face and get outa there! We think the Germans were here to blow up this ship!"

57

Cockroach and Butch ran out onto the deck and started for the rail where they had climbed aboard. Butch turned just in time to see Slug coming out the galley door with at least three pies in his hands. A flash of brilliant light blinded him. The ship shuddered under the force of a huge explosion inside her hold. Beneath Butch's feet the steel deck buckled, and a cargo hatch flew straight up into the air. When he looked again, Slug was gone, and flames were pouring out of the galley.

"Slug!" Butch screamed at the flames as he got to his feet and started toward the burning galley.

Cockroach grabbed his arm, spinning him around. "Ya can't help him!"

"No, let go of me!" Butch cried and swung a wild left hook that caught Cockroach in the mouth. Again, he started running for the flames, but Cockroach tackled him, bringing him down hard onto the deck.

"He's gone, man," Cockroach yelled over the roar of the fire. "He bought it!"

Butch just stared at him.

"Yeah, I know. It's tough, but we gotta get outa here, or we're gonna end up just like him." Another explosion rumbled deep inside the ship, and fountains of flame erupted near the bow. With Cockroach's help, Butch got to the rail. Far below, they could see Merriweather in *Southwind*'s tender.

"You know how to swim?" Butch asked, wiping his nose on his sleeve.

Cockroach looked insulted. "Swim? Why would I know how to swim? I ain't no fish."

Butch handed him a life preserver, which had been hanging on the rail. "Hold on to this!" he said. "Now jump!"

Cockroach turned pale as he looked at the dark water, swirling far, far below. Then he looked at the life preserver. "Yeah, right," he said. "I'll hold on to this. You

58

better believe I'll hold on to this." A pool of burning oil seeped across the deck and flames licked at his heels.

"Go!" Butch yelled, "Right now!"

"All right, all right, I'm going," Cockroach answered, and together they jumped from the burning ship.

Within seconds, Merriweather rowed the tender in close and began pulling the boys out of the water. "We gotta get outa here," Butch gasped as he was pulled over the side. "Slug bought it, and there's a U-boat out there."

Aboard *Southwind,* Stanley had already started the little engine and was motoring toward them. Maisy and Tadpole helped them climb aboard.

"Get us away from here," Merriweather panted as he tied off the tender. "That ship may explode any minute!" Slowly, *Southwind* began to move, heading toward the sinking ship's stern.

"Gunner," Cockroach called as he hurried below, "help me get that box I hid under your bunk." Instantly, Gunner spread his arms and soared off from his position beside Stanley.

"Hey, come back here. I need you to trim sails!" Stanley called after him, but Gunner paid no attention.

"Let the little fruitcake go. I'll help you," Maisy said as she hurried toward the wheel. Flames boiled in the night sky and reflected in deep shades of red and orange on the water as *Southwind* moved slowly past the burning freighter. Billows of stinking black smoke swept down across the schooner's decks and cast strange shadows against her sails. Escaping air bubbled around the freighter's hull. Her stern rose slowly skyward, higher and higher until her monstrous propeller hung exposed above the sea.

Southwind glided past the freighter's stern, and for a moment they could see the clouds on the far horizon. Then the U-boat's long, low silhouette moved suddenly into view, slicing knifelike through the water, and heading straight across *Southwind*'s bow.

"Look out, I think we're going to hit him!" Stanley shrieked.

Sparks's head and shoulders appeared suddenly above one of the hatches. "Hey, what's all the noise up . . . ?" Just then he saw the U-boat. "Uh-oh!" he said, and disappeared again.

Merriweather was running for the wheel. "Turn away, turn away, or you'll sink us!" he yelled. Butch beat him to the wheel and helped Stanley force the big schooner to turn a few more degrees. Merriweather, he noticed out of the corner of his eye, was now leaning against the mast and holding his chest. The U-boat was very close. In the light of the burning freighter, Butch thought he could see someone with a white hat, watching them from the conning tower.

Tadpole burst out of the salon hatch, lugging one of the old rifles. "Gonna kill me some Germans," he vowed, and a second later the gun discharged, knocking him down. "Did I get one? Did I get one?" he asked excitedly as he scrambled to his feet. From the U-boat, machine-gun fire answered him and shattered the night. Bullets whipped through *Southwind*'s sails and sent splinters flying from her masts. One of her antennas hit the water and vanished.

"No, you little twerp," Maisy cursed at Tadpole as she grabbed up the rifle. "You didn't get one . . . you just made him mad enough to hurt somebody." She chambered another round and rested the heavy barrel across the railing as she aimed. The rifle cracked and, on the U-boat conning tower, the white hat suddenly jumped into the air and landed in the water.

"Wow!" Tadpole yelled. "Do it again, do it again!"

The U-boat sped forward, her diesel engines roaring and air hissing from around her hull as she slowly began to submerge. As *Southwind* plowed across her stern, machine-gun fire rattled again, and everyone ducked before they realized the gun was aboard *Southwind,* firing at the U-boat.

"Oh, my," Merriweather gasped weakly. "Where did we get that?"

"Cockroach 'requisitioned' it from the navy," Butch yelled above the roar of battle as he fought to trim a sail. "He's real good at that." The machine gun rattled once more as the U-boat vanished into the night.

The battle ended as quickly as it had begun. *Southwind* sailed on the dark sea. In the distance, the freighter's stern rose higher and then slipped quietly beneath the waves, leaving no trace.

"Stanley," Merriweather said in a weak voice, "stay at the wheel for me . . . I'm not feeling very well."

"Yes, sir," Stanley answered. "Can we get you anything?"

"No, I'm just feeling very tired, I . . ."

His sentence went unfinished as Merriweather collapsed onto the deck and lay very still.

11

"The only thing that I'm certain of is, he hasn't been shot," Stanley said, fighting back his tears. Merriweather lay on his bunk in the captain's cabin, where they had moved him as soon as he fell. After nearly an hour, he still remained unconscious, and his face had turned a stony gray.

"At least he's still breathing," Maisy said. "That's more than we can say for Slug."

"Forget Slug . . . he's gone," Butch snapped. "What we have to do now is sail *Southwind* back into the nearest port where there's a hospital."

"He's right," Stanley nodded.

"Yeah," Cockroach agreed. "And you guys know how to do that, right?"

Stanley nodded. "Bimini Island in the Bahamas is closest. I was there last summer. All we have to do is sail southeast until we sight it."

Maisy looked up from playing with her hands. "They speak English there?" she asked.

"Yes, of course," Stanley answered. "It's a British colony."

"Oh."

"So, shouldn't we call somebody on the radio or something?" Tadpole asked.

"We can't," Sparks reminded them sadly. "The U-boat shot off one of our antennas, and it just happens to be the one for the transmitter. We can hear fine, but we can't send any messages. I'm gonna try to fix it, but I don't know if I can."

Maisy and Tadpole stayed with Merriweather while the others went on deck and trimmed *Southwind*'s sails. No one said much as Stanley took the wheel and pointed the bow south. A hundred miles or so ahead lay Bimini Island. Sparks slipped quietly away to his radio room again. Cockroach and Gunner found the manual which had come with their stolen machine gun. They carried the gun below and began cleaning it. Butch finished coiling down the last of the lines on deck. "Goin' aloft," he said to Stanley and picked up the binoculars.

Alone in the crow's nest, Butch felt the wind on his face and listened to the constant, bubbling rush of water pass *Southwind*'s hull. The sea was dappled with moonlight, and there were stars among the scattered clouds. He realized that nowhere on earth were stars brighter than when viewed from the masthead of a sailing ship, far out at sea. Each one twinkled like cold fire, just inches, it seemed, beyond his reach. It had been many years since tears had touched Butch Hoover's face. Since his father's death, he had buried his feelings deep inside and hardened himself to a world which showed him only cruelty and disappointment. But tonight, alone with the sea and stars, he sat down in the crow's nest and cried for a very long time.

In the captain's cabin, Maisy pulled a blanket up

closer around Merriweather's neck. "He seems like he's sleeping," she said to Tadpole, who was sitting cross-legged on the floor. "I'm going to the kitchen."

"You're supposed to call it the 'galley'," Tadpole corrected, "but I guess it really doesn't matter."

He followed Maisy back through the salon. She noticed the rifle she had fired earlier. Absently, she picked it up and unloaded it. "Here, lock this up where it belongs," she said. "And don't play with it."

Tadpole took the weapon from her. "I didn't know girls could shoot," he said.

"Oh yeah? Well, there's a lot of things you don't know," Maisy snapped. And then, she said in a softer tone, "How ya think I ended up at Greystone?"

"I dunno," Tadpole shrugged.

"I shot my no-good bum of a stepfather, that's how," Maisy said.

A look of total wonder spread over Tadpole's face. "How come?" he asked.

"He hurt my mother," Maisy said and turned away. "And he was gonna hurt me." She hurried into the galley.

Tadpole thought about that for a while as he stood with the rifle in his hands. For as far back as his memory went, he had always just been at one orphanage or another. Although he had often tried, he could never quite imagine what it would be like to be part of a family and have a mother and father, or even a stepfather (whatever that was). *Maybe being part of a family,* he thought, *was kind of like being here, aboard* Southwind.

At sunrise, a string of low islands was visible on the southern horizon. Through the binoculars, Butch could make out the red-tiled roofs of whitewashed houses shining among palm trees in the morning sun. He watched them for so long that he did not notice the ship that steamed up behind him until it was less than a mile away. The sight startled him when he saw the thin, gray bow slicing easily through the waves and saw the gun turrets on her deck.

An odd mixture of feelings swept over him when he saw that she flew the American flag. Merriweather would be taken quickly to a hospital now — that was most important, and something to be happy about. But with that realization came also a tremendous feeling of failure. This had all been his fault. He had run away from the orphanage, he had made the suggestion to Stanley, and then he had convinced the rest of the kids to join him. Now Slug was dead, and the rest of them would all be in a lot of trouble — all because of him.

In a matter of minutes, the Coast Guard cutter had slipped alongside and a doctor was aboard *Southwind,* along with several sailors and a very young-looking lieutenant with pimples on his face. "Who is in charge here?" the lieutenant asked as he looked suspiciously around the deck and saw no grown-ups.

"I — I guess I am, sir," Stanley announced uncertainly. "I'm Captain Merriweather's grandson."

The lieutenant frowned at them. "Do you mean to tell me that old man put to sea with nothing but a bunch of rug rats for a crew?"

"What'd you call me?" Cockroach demanded and kicked the lieutenant in the shins.

The lieutenant howled in pain and then cursed. "Bosun," he yelled at one of the sailors. "Round up these hooligans and get them below." He grabbed Cockroach by his collar and had started below with him when Butch punched him in the stomach.

"Hey, tough guy, pick on somebody your own size!" Butch challenged.

One of the sailors made a grab for Gunner, but the boy slipped between his legs and scurried up the mast, screaming like an airplane all the way. Before things settled down, it had taken nearly twenty minutes to corral

65

all seven kids and get them seated in the salon. The lieutenant pointed to a big, burly sailor. "Now, see that they stay here," he said and stormed out on deck.

Tadpole turned to Maisy, who was seated beside him. "Is he related to the penguins?" he asked.

Late that afternoon, *Southwind* was towed to a dock on Bimini, where an ambulance was waiting to take Merriweather to a hospital. Only Stanley was allowed to go along. The rest were left aboard, and a guard was posted on the gangplank to see that they stayed there.

Cockroach leaned against the mast and chewed on a toothpick as he watched the Coast Guard cutter steam out of the harbor. Butch sat down on the deck beside him and buried his head in his hands. "So," Cockroach asked casually, "where do we go from here?"

"That's a dumb question," Butch groaned. "We got caught. We're all going back to Greystone, and the penguins are gonna tan our hides for runnin' off."

Cockroach spat his toothpick overboard. "What's the biggest thing you ever stole?" he asked after awhile.

Butch laughed bitterly. "A boat," he said without looking up.

"Yeah, that's what I heard. So, maybe you oughta be thinkin' about stealin' this one," Cockroach said as he strolled off with his hands in his pockets.

12

Meyer focused his periscope on a single floating lump, which appeared to be the only remains of the freighter *Orion*. At first it looked to be a broken hatch cover, but as the submerged U-boat moved in closer, he could see that it was something more.

"*Verdammen!*" Meyer cursed and slammed the periscope handles closed. "Down scope, stand by to surface," he ordered and waited impatiently as air hissed from the U-boat's ballast tanks.

"Ten meters, nine, eight, six, three — surface!" an officer called in the eerie red light of the conning tower. Meyer and the other men headed for the ladder. A little water splashed on him as the hatch was thrown open. Fresh, cool air hit his face as he followed the last man up.

From the tiny, cramped space between the periscopes and the conning tower railing, Meyer scanned the ocean — deserted now except for the single bit of wreckage.

"Why haf you again surfaced?" an irritated voice suddenly asked.

Meyer turned slightly to see the dark, shadow-shrouded figure standing beside him. "Ah, Herr Von Sturm," he answered sarcastically. "How nice of our spy to join us. It seems we have a body floating there. I want to have a look at it."

"How nice indeed," Von Sturm echoed, returning the sarcasm as he lit a cigarette. "Had you taken my advice and killed the crew of that freighter, we would have no need to be on the surface again." Von Sturm was very thin with whitish blond hair, which seemed even lighter in the moonlight. He wore a black turtleneck sweater and a wool hat. "But no, you let them row away all safe and sound in their little lifeboats."

"Herr Von Sturm," Meyer said with a sigh, "it is not my wish to survive this war and then be hanged for war crimes. For the moment, at least, the German navy has no orders to murder merchant seamen."

"Your mission requires that I remain undetected, at any cost," Von Sturm insisted.

Meyer laughed grimly. "And so you shall. That is why I must see what we have floating here. We know the freighter's crew got to the boats and was far away before we surfaced to finish off the ship. So this body must have come from that blasted sailboat."

This time, it was Von Sturm who laughed. "Yes, you did look rather funny when they shot off your hat."

"I did not surface to recover my hat," Meyer snapped. "The sailboat, I believe, is being used for some sort of patrol duty. So, I intend to see what I can learn about it."

The freighter, Meyer knew, had gotten off one message on the radio before a round from the deck gun had blown away the radio room. Even after that, she had almost managed to slip away in the dark before Meyer was able to put a torpedo into her. He had waited while her crew had taken to the lifeboats and rowed away toward

68

the American coast. A second torpedo was fired but it had failed to explode, leaving him little choice but to send men aboard with charges to blow her up.

And then, just when everything seemed almost finished, there had been the schooner, sailing up concealed from view behind the freighter, and then taking pot-shots at him.

"Port easy, all stop," Meyer called down the speaking tube to the control room below, and the U-boat swung slowly to the left and eased to a stop. The floating object was pulled aboard.

"It's a body, Captain," Schultz called from the deck. "I think you will want to see it."

Meyer noted a tone of distaste in Schultz's voice, but he shrugged and climbed down from the conning tower, with Von Sturm right behind him.

"It's a child, sir," Schultz said when they arrived. "It was floating on a piece of wreckage."

Meyer raised one eyebrow and turned a flashlight on the body sprawled on the deck at his feet. The face was a mass of red pulp, with odd lumps which were like nothing Meyer had ever seen before.

"It is horrible," Von Sturm said from over his shoulder. "Why not throw it back and let the sharks finish with it?"

"I know it is not possible, Herr Captain," Schultz ventured to say. "But it seems to be still breathing."

"Insane!" Von Sturm answered and knelt for a closer look. As he watched, a bit of the red goo moved, then parted, and exposed an open eye that stared up at him. More of the mess bubbled, and suddenly there was a mouth. He watched, spellbound by the horrible sight as the mouth opened and then belched, spattering his face with nasty red lumps.

Von Sturm jumped backward, lost his balance, and ended up sitting on the deck. Desperately, he tried to wipe the gore from his face with the sleeve of his sweater.

Suddenly, he stopped and sniffed loudly. With his finger, he tasted a bit of the red. A look of total amazement spread across his face as he looked up at Meyer. "Cherries?" he said. "This tastes like cherry pie."

The figure belched again and started to sit up as sailors climbed over each other, trying to get out of the way. "I won't eat no more!" Slug cried. "I promise I won't eat no more!" He wiped cherry pie off his other eye and looked around, slowly realizing where he was. "Hi," he said with a gulp. "An' I won't tell nobody nothin'."

From under his sweater, Von Sturm removed a small, automatic pistol and pointed it at Slug's head. "Wait," Meyer said, gripping Von Sturm's arm none too gently. "I believe I made it quite clear I want to talk to this one."

"I don't know nothin'!" Slug blurted out. "I ain't never knowed nothin'!"

Meyer shrugged. "Very well, shoot him and — "

"I'll talk! I'll tell you anything ya wanna know, anything at all!" Slug yelled all the way as he was hauled down the U-boat's forward hatch. Not until his feet hit the metal grating of the U-boat's floor did he stop and look around.

In the red, night lights, he seemed to be surrounded by a forest of pipes and valves. Dark figures towered above him and moved in the half-light, their faces hidden in shadow. Everywhere were the rumblings of machinery, and the sour odor of diesel oil mixed with sweat burned his nose. "Yuk," he coughed. "Hey, this place smells worse than the orphanage kitchen when they're cookin' liver and pea soup."

A siren wailed through the ship and the hatch slammed shut above them. "Dive! Dive!" sounded somewhere from over a little speaker.

"Hey, wait a minute you guys, what's goin' on here?"

"We are diving. Now, be silent up and wash yourself. The captain wants to talk to you before we shoot you," someone told him in broken English and laughed as they pushed him into a tiny, dark room. The steel door slammed shut, and Slug was alone. Surrounded by more pipes and gauges, he blinked his eyes over and over, trying to adjust them to the dim glow of a single red bulb. With some difficulty, he spotted a metal sink, ran some water into it, and tried to wash the cherry pie from his face.

He was far from finished when the door opened and he was jerked out into the hallway and dragged down to another room where regular white lighting lit up a small table and settee. The captain and the man in the black sweater whom they called "Von Sturm" were there, and a large chart was spread out on the table.

"My name is Captain Meyer, of the German navy," Meyer began, passing a steaming cup across the table. "Coffee?"

"Oh, no, not me," Slug said. "The penguins told me that stuff turns your insides all black and stunts your growth, so you never get any bigger'n I am now an' . . .

Von Sturm looked at Meyer. "Did he say 'penguins'?" he asked.

Meyer ignored him, and asked, "How did you get out there in the ocean?"

Slug thought for a moment. "Well, I don't know exactly. Ya see, I was in the place where they eat, only Captain Merriweather calls it the 'galley.' That's sailor talk for the kitchen."

"Yes, I believe I have heard that term before," Meyer said, smiling a bit.

"Yeah, well, so Cockroach was yellin' at me to hurry up, and then I seen this huge, I mean really big stack of cherry pies. An' they was just sittin' there and there wasn't no one left ta eat 'em. And I ain't et no cherry pie for longer than I can remember, so I grabbed 'em up and ate most of one, and then I was eatin' on another one and . . ." Slug hesitated.

"Either he is insane or he is talking in circles, trying to stall for time," Von Sturm insisted. "Either way, I say we shoot him."

Meyer gave Slug a hard, frowning stare. "I suggest you finish the story very quickly," he said.

"Well, ya see, the next part is what I'm not sure of. I was hurrying to catch up, 'cause Butch said the ship was gonna blow up, and well — next thing I remember, I was in the water, and you guys were dragging me up here, an' talkin' about shootin' me."

Von Sturm grunted and turned to Meyer. "I don't think he knows anything," he said.

Meyer thought for a moment. "What was the name of your ship?" he asked Slug.

"Oh, that's easy. She's the *Southwind*."

A smile spread slowly across Meyer's face. "And the ship I sank was the *Orion*. We heard her very clearly when she sent her SOS. So, you came from that arrogant little schooner who fired on us."

Slug gulped. "I ain't sayin' no more."

"Where was the schooner bound for?" Meyer demanded.

Von Sturm sounded bored. "What does it matter?"

"It interests me. Now, for where was the *Southwind* bound?"

Slug folded his arms and stared at the chart on the table. "I ain't sayin' nothing more!" he insisted.

One of the U-boat's crewmen entered the room. "Message from flotilla, sir," he said and handed the captain a slip of paper.

Meyer looked up at Von Sturm as soon as he read the message. "There has been another delay. Your contacts on shore have radioed that there is too much patrol activity in the area. They are to recontact us within seventy-two hours."

Von Sturm was not happy, but he nodded. "So be it," he said with a sigh.

What d'ya think; you gonna blow up something?" Slug asked.

Von Sturm smiled wickedly. "You Americans think you are so safe and snug, but we are going to bring the war to your doorsteps." He pointed at a penciled "X" on the chart. "In just three days, I will lead a group of saboteurs to begin destroying factories, radio stations, roads, whatever we find," he announced proudly and laid a chart out on the table.

Slug felt suddenly even worse than he had all night. "I wish you hadn't told me that," he groaned. " 'Cause now I know you're gonna kill me!" he felt one of the cherry pies turn over in his stomach and start up toward his throat. A moment later, he vomited all over Von Sturm's chart.

13

With a very large, black Bahamian policeman beside him, Stanley walked along the stone dock to where *Southwind* was moored. At the end of the gangplank, he stopped and stared sadly up at the schooner.

"Be happy, mon," the policeman said with a smile. "Doctor says your grandfather going be all right. And you and your friends shall all be returning home very soon."

"Let me tell them," Stanley said quietly and walked up the gangplank. He met Butch on the deck and avoided his eyes as he said, "Tell everyone we're having a meeting."

They gathered in *Southwind*'s cockpit, shaded from the sun by a canvas awning they had rigged over the main boom. When everyone was seated, Stanley took a deep breath and said, "Grandfather — I mean, Captain Merriweather — is going to be okay."

"All right!" Tadpole cheered.

"Yeah, that's great!" the others chorused.

"But he has to stay here in the hospital for several weeks," Stanley continued, "and it looks like he won't ever be doing any more sailing. He has given *Southwind* to the Coast Guard, at least for the rest of the war."

"So, what's *he* for?" Cockroach asked, pointing at the policeman on the dock.

"Since we still have guns and explosives on board, there will be a guard here all the time." He paused and looked around at the young faces. "There is a ship due here in a couple of days which will take all of us back to the States."

In unison, the young faces wilted. "Aw heck," Tadpole said. He kicked at the cockpit floor, and Gunner made a sputtering noise, like a sick engine.

Maisy stood up. "I don't wanna go," she said.

"Smart broad," Cockroach mocked her sarcastically. "She don't want to go back."

"Nobody ever wanted to go back to Greystone," Butch echoed. "And I ain't goin'." He looked around the harbor. "I'm stowin' away on the first ship that anchors here."

"Why go lookin' for a ship, when you're sittin' on one?" Cockroach suggested with a sly smile.

Butch threw up his hands and stomped over to the rail. "We can't just take *Southwind*. And even if we did, what the heck would we do with her?"

"You ever read this?" Cockroach asked him, holding up a tattered old book. "It's called *Captain Blood*."

Stanley made a grab for the book and missed. "Hey," he said. "You got that out of my cabin!"

"Yeah, so what?"

"So when did you start reading?" Sparks laughed.

"I read," Cockroach responded sharply, staring at Stanley with a crooked smile, "when I got something to learn from it. Now the story here, it's about this guy who gets accused of something he didn't do, so he steals a ship and turns pirate."

75

Stanley objected immediately. "That is completely crazy."

"For you, it's crazy," Sparks cut in, pointing a finger at Stanley. "Because you're not going back to a lousy old orphanage and sleep in a room full of crazy kids."

Stanley stood up and stomped one foot on the deck. "I don't want to hear another word about it. That is the craziest idea I ever heard!" He looked around and was answered only with silent faces. "Okay," he said. "Let's forget it. Now, the policeman says we are free to visit the island if we like. So I suggest shore leave for all hands."

With somewhat less enthusiasm than his own, the others followed Stanley ashore. The policeman looked up as they passed by. "So, you are going to look over our beautiful island?"

"Yeah," Tadpole groaned. "We're going to see if ya got any orphanages here that need kids."

The policeman looked puzzled. "We have no orphans here," he said, but pointed out at the harbor, where a large ship flying the British flag had anchored during the night. "Now there, that ship just come from England, and she's full of 'em."

They all looked out at the great, gray-painted liner. She was much larger than the freighter they had boarded, and her decks were crowded with people. Little wisps of black smoke were rising from four tall smokestacks, and she appeared to be very fast.

"Full of orphans?" Cockroach asked doubtfully. "Aw, come on, you're pullin' my leg."

"It the truth, mon. Germans is bombing England every day, so they send all the children away from the cities. Some they send out to the country, but a bunch of them, mostly the poor ones and the orphans, they send to the United States until the war is over. Now that ship, she's the *Providence* out of Liverpool, and she's sailin' for Louisiana tonight. Got about a hundred or so orphans aboard her, I hear."

76

The policeman watched the ragged little group as they stared out at the anchored ship. "I hope none of them kids end up where we come from," Tadpole sighed. Then slowly, they all walked off down the dock.

For the rest of the day, they wandered about the island and, for everyone but Stanley, it was a place like nothing they had ever seen. White sand beaches stretched away from palm groves to meet an ocean so clear that it was almost invisible. West of town was a well which, so an old man told them, had once been used by pirates. Along the waterfront were a few shops, but of course they had no money, so they only stared in the windows at silver jewelry, bright flowered clothing, and polished sea shells.

Sometime around noon, Cockroach wandered off by himself. With his shoes off and hanging by their laces over his shoulder, he strolled along the white sand beach. There were several small children playing in the ocean, and a girl about his own age sat watching them from the shade of a palm tree.

"Good morning," she greeted him from under the wide brim of a straw hat.

"Hi, ya," Cockroach returned. "You from around here?"

The girl smiled, and Cockroach melted. Eyes of hazel green sparkled as he approached. Her hair was a deep brown and hung far down across the shoulders of her loose, white dress. "Oh, no," she said, "I'm from London, sailing aboard the *Providence*."

"Then you're — you're one of them orphans?"

She shook her head and brown curls moved on her forehead. "Actually no," she said. "My family lives in London." In answer to Cockroach's questioning frown, she explained. "When the children were being sent away, I could have simply moved to our country home, but I wanted to be of some help for the war effort. So I came

77

along to take care of these little ones," she nodded at the children splashing in the ocean. "They're all orphans."

"Yeah," Cockroach said thoughtfully. "I guess that's kind of what I'm doin' too — helpin' the war effort."

"Really?" She sounded doubtful.

"Yeah, we're in the Coast Guard, sort of. We come in on that sailboat. Been out huntin' U-boats."

"The gray schooner? She's quite beautiful, and you must be very brave."

Cockroach swelled with sudden pride and stuck out his chest until it strained the buttons on his shirt. "Well, yeah, it goes with the territory, I guess," he said, shuffling his feet in the sand.

"By the way," the girl added, extending her hand, "my name is Lauren."

"I'm — well, my friends call me 'Cockroach'."

She hesitated a moment, and then shook his hand. "An — an interesting name," she said. For the next hour they talked of many things. When it was time for her to go, Cockroach said, "Feels like I've known ya for a long time."

Lauren smiled and stared deeply into his eyes. "Yes," she agreed, "I believe it does."

Cockroach spent the rest of the afternoon alone. Evening was near before he rejoined the others, and they all strolled back along the dock where *Southwind* was berthed. By then, the *Providence* had already sailed and was out of sight.

The policeman was still there, dozing in the shade of a palm tree. "Good evening," he greeted them with a yawn and got to his feet. "How did you like our island?"

"Pretty nice," Cockroach answered. "Wish't we was stayin' a while." The others agreed as they filed aboard the schooner just as the sun was setting.

An hour later, they all sat down for supper at the big table in the salon. Cockroach sniffed at the steaming pot that Maisy set on the table. "Hey," he said, "this don't smell too bad. You cook it?"

"Well, no," Maisy admitted. "Actually, you won't believe this, but — "

"I cooked it," Tadpole interrupted proudly as bowls were being filled. "It's Mulligan stew. That's what hobos eat."

"This is good," Sparks said, after taking a cautious bite. "Where'd you learn to cook?"

Tadpole shrugged. "Learned it from a guy I met one time when I ran away."

"So it looks like we finally got us a cook," Butch said. "Nice goin', Tadpole."

Maisy cast her eyes slowly around the group and then looked away. "Kinda like a family, ain't it?" she said, but no one answered her.

After a while, Butch sighed and pushed his bowl away. "Of course it really doesn't matter now, does it?"

"Yeah," Cockroach replied. "We gotta decide what we're gonna do." He looked around the room, but no one seemed eager to suggest anything. "What is this? You guys want to go back to Greystone?"

Maisy stood up and started collecting dishes. "I don't see where we got no choice in the matter."

"Sure we do," Cockroach insisted. "We're here, on some island that the United States don't even own. We got this sailboat under us. Now, there's gotta be somewhere in this rotten world where half-a-dozen kids can go and nobody's gonna ask no questions about where they came from." He picked up a chart and dropped it on the table. "So, where?"

"This ain't our boat," Butch said.

Cockroach spread open the chart. "So, we don't need it forever. We just need it for long enough to get somewhere. Then the Coast Guard can have it for the rest of the war. After that, Stanley can have his old boat and sail it back to the yacht club, or wherever it is he comes from." Cockroach leaned against the wall and stared knowingly at Stanley. "Of course, now, ol' goody-goody Stanley there might not really be in such a big hurry to get home."

Stanley's face went pale as he glared up at Cockroach. "What are ya talkin' about?" Butch demanded.

Cockroach took a couple of quick steps across the salon. "Well, by now, I figure Stanley's mommy and daddy probably found out he got himself expelled from that fancy boarding school he goes to." He flipped his finger at the crest on Stanley's blazer.

Stanley came off his seat swinging. His right went wild, but his left caught Cockroach in the stomach and doubled him over. Before another punch could be thrown, Butch had stepped between them. "Knock it off!" he ordered, pulling Cockroach to his feet. "Now, what are you talkin' about?"

Cockroach gasped for breath. "Not bad . . . didn't figure . . . ol' Stanley there . . . had it in him." From out of his pocket, he pulled a folded letter and handed it to Butch. "I found this. It was hid in that book I was readin'."

Butch took the letter and started to read it, when Stanley suddenly blurted out, "It says I was expelled from school for cheating on a test! I stole the letter out of our mailbox and hid it in the book."

"And no one knows about it?" Butch asked.

"Grandfather does not. By now, I'm sure the school has contacted my parents."

"You had to know they'd find out," Maisy said.

Stanley jammed his hands in his pockets and paced nervously. "I figured maybe if I got out on *Southwind,* and we really did something important for the war, then that would make up for it — I guess."

"Well, we can still do something for the war," Butch insisted. "Let's take *Southwind* back to her patrol area and do what we were supposed to do in the first place."

80

Sparks shook his head. "Won't work," he said. "Did you guys forget that we got our transmitter antenna shot off? We can receive messages, but we can't transmit. So we couldn't report anything, even if we saw it."

"Can't you fix it or something?" Maisy asked.

"If I could fix it, I'd already done it," Sparks said. "I tried hooking up to the antenna that's still on the mast and I blew out what was left of the transmitter." He walked back to the radio room, flipped on the receiver, and listened to the static for a while. He had leaned over to tune in a station that played music, when a desperate voice suddenly blared from the speaker.

"This is liner *Providence,* attacked by U-boat — burning!"

Instinctively, Sparks swung the direction-finding antenna and wrote down the bearing, a second before the voice went dead.

Cockroach burst into the radio room. "We gotta get to 'em!" he yelled at Sparks.

Stanley had followed him and now stood in the hallway outside. "Don't be silly. All we have to do is tell the policeman on the dock."

"Oh, yeah, that's a great idea, except for one little thing," Cockroach continued to rage. "There ain't no boats on this island, except us!"

"Then he'll have someone radio the navy!" Stanley insisted.

Cockroach grabbed the paper Sparks had written on and thrust it into Stanley's hand. "Yeah, you do that," he said, and watched as Stanley hurried out on deck. For a few moments, everyone was silent.

"Cockroach is right," Maisy said finally. "They're orphans like us. We should help 'em."

" 'Course we should," Butch added. "So what are we waitin' for?"

Stanley came hurrying back into the salon. "Waiting for what?" he asked.

81

Butch looked him straight in the eye. "We're takin' *Southwind,* and we're going out after the liner. Don't try to stop us."

Stanley stared at them for a few seconds. "I'm with you," he said with a sigh. "So let's get out of here before that policeman comes back."

In a surprisingly short time, they had started the engine and cast off the dock lines. *Southwind's* sails were already set when they slipped past the ancient stone lighthouse at the harbor entrance and headed out onto the dark sea.

14

U-132 had surfaced during the last fading glow of twilight and set course for the United States coast. Only minutes earlier, her sonar operator had picked up the distant growl of a ship's engine. "She is too far away to tell what she is, or even what course she is on," he had reported.

"We have no time to chase her tonight." Meyer had shrugged at Schultz. "Von Sturm's contacts report that they are ready for him, so we must get into position as soon as possible." He climbed the ladder up through the U-boat's main hatch and onto the conning tower. "And make sure the lookouts are awake," he told Schultz. "I am going to run fast, and try to stay on the surface all night."

It was a somewhat dangerous move, Meyer knew. On the surface, the U-boat could not use her sonar, and so was unable to listen for other ships. Also, with her diesels roaring, and driving her through the seas at over sixteen knots, she would leave a white, glowing wake which

A look inside a German U-Boat

U-132

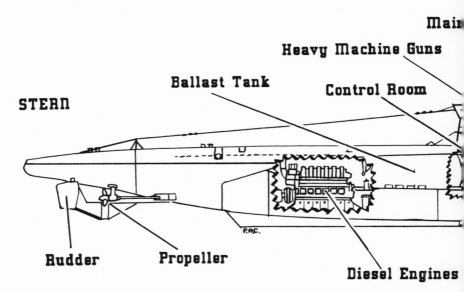

Main

Heavy Machine Guns

Ballast Tank

Control Room

STERN

Rudder

Propeller

Diesel Engines

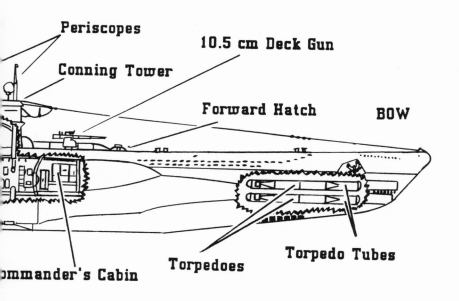

Periscopes

Conning Tower

10.5 cm Deck Gun

Forward Hatch

BOW

Commander's Cabin

Torpedoes

Torpedo Tubes

might be visible for miles. All these things Meyer knew, but the sooner he reached the coast, the sooner he would be rid of Von Sturm. For that, he would take some risks.

Meyer checked his lookouts once again, and then scanned the horizon himself. He felt the vibration of his ship beneath him and found the steady rhythm of engines and sea pleasant.

And then, Meyer thought, *there was still the problem of that strange, disgusting child who insisted on calling himself "Slug."* Von Sturm, of course, was demanding that he be killed. For the last twenty-four hours, Meyer had tried to think of some other way. The problem remained that the boy already knew too much. He knew that a saboteur was to be landed on the U.S. coast. He had even seen the chart which showed the location at which he was to go ashore, although Meyer doubted that he had read or understood it.

Schultz, on the other hand, considered him harmless. "Put him ashore on some deserted island," he had suggested. "You have heard him talk. Who in the world would pay any attention to what he says?"

Von Sturm would never approve, Meyer was certain. He looked at his watch. Perhaps there was still time to think of something.

"Ship! Bearing green-four-O!" The lookout's cry shattered his thoughts.

"Dive! Dive!" Meyer ordered as the lookouts scurried like rats down the hatch. Meyer looked over his shoulder and saw the ship. At once he knew that the lookout had seen her too late. There was a chance that she might have spotted the U-boat's wake or caught the silhouette of her conning tower against the horizon. He cursed as he dropped through the hatch, pulling it shut behind him, only seconds before the U-boat slipped beneath the seas.

Meyer trimmed his boat at periscope depth, then ordered the scope up and focused on the ship. *"Mein Gott!"* he whispered. "She is a liner."

86

"Probably carrying American soldiers?" Schultz suggested, opening a large book full of ship pictures.

Through the periscope, Meyer described the liner. "I make her about six thousand tons; she has four stacks, very sharp bow — "

"I've got her, sir. She's British — the *Providence*." As Schultz spoke, the ship began to change course, turning away to the south.

Meyer cursed and slammed the periscope shut. "Right full rudder, ahead full! Torpedo room, standby bow tubes," he ordered, and then turned to Schultz. "She's seen us, but we still may get a shot at her."

Deep below in the U-boat's hull, Slug heard the dive alarm screech and almost fell on the floor as the boat started down. For hours, he had been sitting forlornly on the toilet, which happened to be the only place to sit in the tiny room where he had been locked up.

When the boat again became quiet and level, he got up and began to beat on the steel door just as he had done off and on all day. "Hey, out there," he yelled. "I wanna come out now. It's dark in here, and it stinks. Come on, let me out!"

Much to his surprise, the door suddenly opened. Von Sturm dragged him out into the hallway and slapped him across the face. "Don't you know how to be quiet?" he cursed as he dragged Slug along.

"Torpedos, *los!*" Meyer's voice ordered from somewhere ahead, and the swishing rush of escaping air echoed through the ship. For the next two minutes, no one aboard the U-boat moved or spoke as a spread of four torpedos ran toward the *Providence*. Then two dull explosions rumbled in the distance, and everyone began to cheer — everyone except Slug.

Slug found himself being dragged and pushed up into the conning tower, where Meyer was again at the periscope. "Any survivors?" Von Sturm asked.

"I think not. There was a large explosion, and she

went down too fast," Meyer answered. "I see only a few bodies."

"Excellent," Von Sturm said and pointed at Slug. "One more will not be noticed."

Avoiding Slug's eyes, Meyer stared into the periscope. Then he nodded his head. Von Sturm was right. One more body among the floating dead, no one would ever suspect. He took a deep breath and released it. "Stand by to surface!" he ordered.

Floating oil burned on the sea and colored it with splotches of orange. Great black clouds of billowing smoke rolled across the U-boat's deck as Slug was pulled out onto the conning tower. Two crewmen were working a spotlight back and forth across the water. Occasionally, it picked up some bit of floating debris or a burned body.

Meyer turned to face Von Sturm. "Very well, get it done," he said. Von Sturm smiled and drew his pistol. "Not here, you idiot!" Meyer cursed. "Take him down on the deck."

"Hey now, wait a minute, guys. I know we can think up somethin' better'n this. I told ya I won't tell nobody nothin'!" Slug cried as he was pulled along. As they passed the twin heavy machine guns mounted just aft of the conning tower, someone called out, "Lifeboat, off the starboard bow!"

Meyer cursed loudly as the spotlight beam fell on a single, overloaded lifeboat. It moved slowly from out of the smoke, heading toward the U-boat. A wave of sudden nausea swept over Meyer as the lifeboat came alongside. At the tiller was a girl dressed in a long, flowing nightgown, and the lifeboat was crowded with children. Like the girl, most wore night clothes and one even carried a teddy bear.

"Von Sturm," Meyer yelled. "Halt."

Von Sturm laughed as he pushed Slug away and climbed up behind one of the machine guns. "It is too late now, Captain. They have seen us." With a loud metallic clunk, he cocked the weapon. "I do not wish to hang as a spy because of a few Englander children." As he aimed at the lifeboat, a sudden pain shot up his leg, and Von Sturm looked down in time to see Slug taking a bite out of his ankle. The German kicked hard, but Slug held on like a terrier. He lost his balance, fell backward, and barely caught himself on the gunmount railing. Again, Von Sturm kicked, finally breaking Slug's hold and knocking him away. Von Sturm staggered back to the machine gun and put the lifeboat in his sights.

Slug jumped from below, got both hands on the barrel, and swung there, pulling it down and away from the lifeboat. "Get away from here, you kids out there!" Slug yelled at the top of his voice. "They're gonna shoot you!" Other arms grabbed at him as more crewmen reached the conning tower. Fists rained down on him until he lost his grip on the machine gun barrel and landed on the steel deck. Somehow he managed to get to his feet and start running. Behind him, he heard the gun open fire. The last thing he remembered was tripping over something and falling forward, over the rail and down, down toward the black water below.

15

All that at first appeared to remain of the British liner *Providence* were little pools of burning oil, drifting on a dark and restless sea. It was not until dawn had begun to streak the eastern sky with shades of pink and blue that Slug fully realized that, somehow, he was still alive. How long he had clung to the shattered piece of overturned lifeboat, he had no idea.

The sky lightened slowly, and the first rays of morning sun splashed gold on the bottoms of a few scattered clouds. Strange-looking things were bobbing in the water all around him, and the stench of burned flesh sickened him. Bodies, he realized, they were bodies — burned and blackened almost beyond recognition. He kicked out wildly at one which brushed against him. "I don't wanna be here!" he screamed and tried to climb higher onto the ruined lifeboat. He heard breathing beside him and realized that he was not alone. With painful effort, he turned his head to the other side.

"Don't thrash around so much," a girl's voice said

weakly. "There's sharks all about." She wore the tattered remains of a white nightgown. Long, brown hair, which might once have held a hint of curl, hung in soaked ringlets about her oil-blackened face. Slug realized that she was the girl he had seen at the lifeboat's tiller, just before . . . he turned away as the memory of it all came back to him.

"I don't understand how you got aboard that U-boat, but I believe you saved my life," she said in a weak whisper. "Thank you."

"We the only ones still alive?" Slug asked.

"I think so — don't move, there's a shark right behind you!"

"Oooh nooo!" Slug wailed and gritted his teeth but somehow managed to hold still. Very slowly, he turned his head until he could squint over his shoulder and see a black fin slicing through the water. "Go away, shark. I ain't no good ta eat! Nothin' that's ugly as me could be good to eat! Not even spinach, an' spinach is real ugly!"

"They're attracted to movement," the girl whispered, "so you must stay very still."

"I'm still," Slug whispered quickly, trying to convince himself. "I'm so still, I'm just like an ol' rock." The shark passed and then circled back toward the girl. Only now, there was not one fin, but two. "Climb up higher," Slug whispered and pulled on her arm. She climbed, but as she did, the broken lifeboat just sank deeper into the water.

"It's not big enough to support both of us," she said, and a tiny, gasping scream escaped her lips. "Oh, God," she whispered, "it touched my leg!" She glanced at the fin. "Now they're coming back!"

For reasons Slug would never fully understand, he suddenly found himself pushing away from the lifeboat and splashing wildly about in the water. "Come on, sharks," he yelled, "I'm over here, ya big, fat, stupidlookin' fish!"

91

Terror blazed in the girl's eyes as she stared at him. "Come back here! What are you doing?" The fins turned, circled once, and then headed for Slug. "Please!" she pleaded as Slug watched the fin head straight for him.

For a moment he saw the shark's gray back break the ocean's surface directly in front of him. Something hit the water hard. The shark rolled, showing a double line of razorlike teeth. Slug felt nothing, but all around him, the water was turning red. "I'm dead! I been ate by a shark! I'm dead an' I just don't know it yet!" he cried.

"You ain't dead, ya jerk!" another voice called to him. He looked around. The first thing he saw was *Southwind*'s bow, slicing through the water toward him. Then he saw Maisy, perched on the bowsprit and sighting a rifle. Again she fired and a second shark rolled over and headed for the bottom, leaving a trail of blood.

Butch was at the rail, throwing a rope, which hit Slug in the face. "Hang on!" he yelled.

A few minutes later, both Slug and the girl were pulled onto *Southwind*'s deck. Slug sat with his back against the main mast, coughing and spitting up sea water.

Sparks came up on deck and stopped short. "Slug!" he said. "Where'd you come from? You're supposed to be dead! And who's she?"

"Her name's Lauren," Cockroach said as he knelt beside the girl. "I met her on the island yesterday."

"Is she okay, or what?" Maisy asked.

"I don't know," Cockroach said, touching her hand. "She ain't said nothing."

Maisy pushed past them. "Of course she ain't said nothin'. She's scared half ta death, with all you apes standin' around starin' at her. Hey! Tadpole, get her a blanket. Come on! Move!"

For the next quarter-hour, Slug told them everything that had happened since the explosion aboard the freighter had blown him into the water.

"And then the men on the U-boat just shot 'em all?" Stanley asked when he had finished.

Slug nodded. "Yeah, I guess."

Lauren spoke at last. "The *Providence* caught fire as soon as she was hit." Her voice was like a hollow echo as she stared out at the sea. "I managed to get a few of the younger children into one of the lifeboats. Some of them were injured, and I thought the U-boat would help us, so I steered for it, and then they started shooting and — " She buried her face in her hands and cried until Maisy helped her below deck.

A quiet state of shock settled over the rest of the crew, and for several minutes no one spoke. With sails flapping, *Southwind* drifted aimlessly among the floating bodies.

Tadpole sat on a hatch cover, jabbing into the wood with a butcher knife over and over again. "No good Germans," he kept saying. Gunner had made airplane noises and climbed up somewhere in the rigging.

Stanley, Butch, and Sparks were in the cockpit when Cockroach sat down beside them. "We gotta do something," Butch said.

"Yeah," Stanley nodded. "Go back, and let everyone know how bad we messed things up."

"We oughta go kill that U-boat," Tadpole said and drove the butcher knife into the hatch again.

"Yeah, right," Stanley answered sadly. "That's real smart."

Butch scratched his chin. "Maybe it is."

"I'm listenin'," Cockroach said, perking up a little.

"Slug said he saw a map while he was on the U-boat, and it showed where they was goin' to put some sort of spy ashore."

"So what?" Stanley groaned.

"So, let's get Slug to look at our map, and see if he can figure out where the U-boat is going."

With little enthusiasm, they all filed below and laid

out the big chart of the United States east coast. "Okay, Slug," Butch said, "anything there look familiar?"

Slug screwed his face into a monsterlike frown and squinted his eyes into little slits as he ran his finger along the coastline. "There was these funny little bumpy places, kinda like this, 'cept bigger, an' fatter. Then I remember a wavy little blue line that run off up that way. And then they had this "X" on the chart but it was farther on down." As Slug talked, Gunner walked quietly into the salon and sat down to watch.

"A river," Stanley prompted. "That would be the symbol for a river."

Slug continued. "Then there was some little round thing-a-ma-jigs sitting out in the ocean, just a little bit."

"Islands."

"There it is!" Slug was suddenly excited. "That's it, I found it, it's right there!"

Stanley looked closely at the chart. "Dolphin Beach?" he said thoughtfully. "Why there?"

"Because there's a big factory there that makes airplane engines," Sparks announced. "I read about it in *Science and Mechanics* magazine last month."

"So, can we get there in time ta catch 'em?" Cockroach asked.

Butch scratched his head. "Get there maybe. It's not all that far away. But what do ya think we're gonna do then?"

"Run over 'em and sink 'em!" Tadpole suggested angrily.

"Smart, real smart!" Stanley replied. "If we ran into a U-boat, we'd be the ones to get sunk."

"Sparks is smart," Tadpole insisted. "He can figure out something to blow up that old U-boat."

All eyes fell suddenly on Sparks. "Hey, wait a minute now. Just because I set the orphanage on fire a couple of times, and I can knock out lights, that don't mean I can handle something this big," he insisted. But then, he

94

began to think. "Of course, we still got the grenades and that other stuff Cockroach stole from the navy."

"What other stuff?" Stanley demanded. "I didn't know about anything else."

Cockroach lifted up one of the settee cushions and pulled out a canvas bag with a shoulder strap on it. "I got a dozen of 'em. Some sailor I heard talkin' called 'em 'satchel charges'." He shrugged.

Sparks took one of the satchels and opened it. "Hmmm," he noted, "very interesting. There's a bunch of explosives in here."

"So, can you do anything with 'em?" Butch sounded anxious.

Sparks thought for a moment. "Maybe, but whatever I do, it's probably gonna blow us up too." He looked around the room. "Of course, that wouldn't be no great loss to the world."

"We gotta get Lauren outa here first — she's got no part in this," Cockroach insisted.

"Yeah, and Maisy too; she's a girl — well, sort of," Tadpole said.

"Forget it, twerp. I'm stayin', an' you guys ain't big enough to stop me." They all turned to see Maisy standing at the doorway. Beside her was Lauren, barefoot and dressed in oversized sailor's dungarees.

"And as far as I am concerned," Lauren said with quivering lips, "I believe I have as big a part in this as any of you. Those were *my friends* whose bodies the sharks are having for breakfast."

Gunner stood up and took his hands out of his pockets. "I think we should try to do it," he said and walked out on deck. Only this time, he did not act like an airplane.

16

A little squall of warm rain pattered across *Southwind*'s deck and then hurried off to the west, leaving a faint rainbow in the western sky. The sweet, fresh scent that it left behind cleaned away much of the lingering stench of burned oil and flesh. Cockroach breathed in deeply and looked up at the midday sky, where a single gull circled lazily above the masthead. It occurred to him that he had never really paid much attention to pleasant little things like birds and the sky before. Now, of course, it was almost too late. With a sigh, he turned his attention back to the job at hand.

"This is the last one," he called as he lowered a satchel charge down the forward hatch, where Sparks was busy packing them tightly against the bow planks. "You think this is gonna be enough?"

"How would I know?" Sparks grumbled. "I never did this before." He sat huddled in the tiny compartment that held *Southwind*'s anchor chain and looked at the thirty-odd pounds of high explosives packed around him.

With his sleeve, he wiped at the steady stream of sweat which ran down his face. Although he had no idea how much explosive it would take to blow up a U-boat, he was pretty sure that there was more than enough here to blow up *Southwind* and everyone aboard her.

Only one detail remained, and he concentrated on how to solve it. They had all agreed that if they could find the U-boat, and if they could get close enough to ram *Southwind* into it, then their escape would have to be made in *Southwind*'s tender. So some method was needed to explode the charges after they were safely away. The satchel charges were designed to be fired electrically, using a little box with a plunger on it, and Sparks had found enough wire to run all the way back to the cockpit. But, unless he figured out something better, whoever set off the charges was going to get blown up with them.

"There's gotta be some way. I still got the grenades . . . maybe I can do something with them," Sparks mumbled as he crawled out and headed back to the radio room to study the problem some more. In the salon, he passed Butch and Stanley. They were sitting at the table and reading a navy manual, while they looked at the chart.

"You think Slug got the position wrong?" Stanley was asking.

"Slug could get anything wrong," Sparks commented. "What's the matter now?

"We been readin' about U-boats," Butch said, pointing at the manual. "According to this book, a U-boat's gotta have over a hundred feet of water under him in order to dive without hitting bottom."

"Yeah, so?"

"So, according to this chart, he's only gonna have about sixty when he drops off that spy."

Sparks shrugged. "Yeah, that could be. The captain figures he'll sneak in on the surface at night, and be gone before morning, so he'd never need to submerge."

"Yes and besides that," Stanley added, "he's going to

be in between these two islands, where he won't have much room to maneuver."

"That might help us," Sparks said, and continued aft to the radio room.

Maisy passed him in the hallway and opened the door to one of the cabins. Inside, she found Lauren standing in front of a mirror. Tears were running down the English girl's face as she touched one of the bruises on her cheek.

"That ain't nothin' to cry about," Maisy said as she entered. "My lousy stepfather used to give me worse than that, just 'cause he felt like it. Here, I brought you some salve from the medicine chest. It'll clear that up in no time."

"I want to die," Lauren said quietly as she stared into the mirror.

For a moment, Maisy could think of no reply. *Dying,* she thought, *that must be what everyone aboard was thinking about, but no one had dared to say it.*

"Come on," Maisy said quickly, "ain't nobody gonna die here. We're just gonna knock off that U-boat. Then you'll be safe in the U.S.A." Lauren ignored her, and so she took a couple of steps to the edge of the bunk.

"Cockroach says you ain't no orphan," Maisy continued. "Says you got a family an' all back in England?"

Lauren only nodded.

"So if anybody deserves to come out of this alive, I figure it's you. I mean, you got a real home to go back to when this war's over. The rest of us? — Heck, we'll never amount ta — "

Lauren turned on her suddenly. "Those children! I was supposed to take care of them!" she cried. "They were my responsibility, and I got them all killed!"

Maisy opened the salve bottle. "This is a war," she said. "It don't make no sense, but it's a war and people are gettin' killed every day. You did the best you could."

She spread a bit of salve on Lauren's cheek, and stared at her for a moment. "I just wish't I was pretty like you."

Lauren choked on her tears, "You — you are pretty," she said.

Maisy shook her head and wiped on more salve. "Not me, and I ain't smart neither. I'm just a bimbo, like my mother was."

"Your mother," Lauren asked, "what happened to her?"

"They took me away from her. Said she wasn't no fit mother." Maisy hesitated and bit her lip. "Then last year, some man she met in a bar went and stabbed her to death." She handed Lauren the salve bottle and stood up. "Here, finish this and shut up, before you get me cryin' or somethin'," she said and walked out.

From the galley came the odors of cooking food. Tadpole had found a tall, white chef's hat and was busily kneading dough on the table. "Bread?" Maisy asked as she walked in, wiping her eyes on her sleeve. "Where'd you learn . . . ?" Before he could answer, she added, "I know, from a hobo."

"Naw," Tadpole answered. "I used to watch the penguins. It's real easy."

"Bread," Maisy grumbled and sat down. "The kid can cook anything, and I can't even boil water without messin' it up."

"So what?" Tadpole asked and punched at the dough again. "Cookin's easy, but you're really neat — you can shoot better'n Dale Evans." He looked at her seriously for a moment. "Ya know, you'd be good to have for a big sister."

Maisy gave him a tired smile. "Okay, kid. I'll make you a deal. I'll teach you to shoot, and you can teach me to cook."

"Yeah, great!"

"Now, put your bread in the oven, and get us a couple

of rifles," Maisy sighed. "I'm afraid you're gonna need to shoot, long before I'm gonna need to cook."

U-132 lay silent and motionless on the ocean floor. Tiny beads of perspiration covered Meyer's face as he listened nervously to constant "ping-ping" of the enemy sonar. Four hundred feet above him on the surface, an American destroyer was circling, while its sonar probed electronically through the depths below, for some telltale sign that the U-boat was still there.

Meyer cursed himself. Von Sturm was still aboard. They should have put him ashore the previous night, but once again, they had taken chances, and run on the surface too fast and too long. Only this time, it had been a warship which had popped suddenly up over the horizon, instead of a helpless liner. He looked at his watch and cursed again. At best, this delay would cost him twenty-four precious hours. He smiled grimly. At worst, the destroyer would drop a depth charge on top of him and blow them all to bits.

"Propeller noises fading," his own sonar operator reported in a whisper.

The destroyer was moving off. Perhaps it had given up the search, and was leaving. Perhaps it was only moving away to wait quietly until, sooner or later, the U-boat surfaced.

Von Sturm mounted the conning tower ladder. "How much longer?" he whispered.

"One hour. Until it is dark," Meyer answered. "Then, if the destroyer is gone, I may get you to your meeting place tonight."

"I cannot be late again," Von Sturm insisted. "My people ashore will try again tonight, but they will not keep waiting forever."

Meyer cocked an ear at the fading sounds of the destroyer. "If he finds us, no one will need to wait for any of us," he whispered with a wicked sneer.

The minutes dragged by. Inside the U-boat, the common odors became stronger. Diesel oil and sweat mingled with the smell of rancid cabbage from the galley. An hour passed and breathing became more difficult as the oxygen inside the U-boat began to be used up. Meyer checked his watch and waited another thirty minutes. Then, with a deep breath, he ordered, "Bring her up slowly. Periscope depth. Gun crew, stand by for surface action."

In submarine school Meyer had often been told that even on the surface, a U-boat stood a fair chance against a destroyer. Destroyers had little armor — a fact which had given them the nickname of "tin can." The U-boat's 10.5 cm deck gun was a better weapon than anything the destroyer carried, and its crew could fire faster. All of this, Meyer had been told many times, but he hoped that he would never have to find out if it was correct.

The submarine rose slowly toward the surface. At thirty feet, Meyer raised the periscope and swung it quickly around the dark horizon. There were clouds in the eastern sky and a thin, gray mist lay on the sea. There was no sign of the destroyer. At last, he relaxed a little. "All clear," he said. "Surface!"

Only fifty miles of ocean lay between his U-boat and the United States coast. Before dawn, he would send Von Sturm on his merry way, and be back into the safety of deep water.

17

During the late afternoon, Stanley had climbed into the crow's nest with the binoculars and spotted the distant coast as well as the two islands which showed on the chart. Now, as sunset approached, they made their final preparations.

"We'll tow the tender from here on," Butch said as he played out some more rope and watched the tender bobbing along in *Southwind*'s wake. "This way it'll be faster for us to get into it when . . ." He hesitated as he tied off the line to a stern cleat, "When the time comes."

"Yes," Stanley added and looked at Maisy. "You and Lauren will go first, and then Tadpole. He's the youngest."

Maisy glared at him but said nothing. Lauren just stared through him, and then looked out at the tender and the rope which held it.

Slug burped. "Looks like it's gonna be awful crowded in there," he noted and stuffed another slice of bread in his mouth.

Butch poked him in the stomach. "So stop eatin' so much, or there ain't gonna be no room for nothing but your fat gut."

Lauren started forward but then stopped beside Slug, and put her hand on his shoulder. "I never thanked you for what you did when the sharks came," she said and kissed him on the forehead. As the others stared with open mouths, Slug blushed a brilliant red.

Lauren ignored them and made her way forward, to where Cockroach stood at the wheel, steering toward the sunset. "I'll relieve you for a while," she said.

"You know how to do this?" Cockroach asked, surprised.

"Quite well, actually. Back in England my family has always owned sailing boats." Cockroach handed over the wheel and sat down beside her. For a while they said nothing as the sun sank out of sight and the horizon changed quickly from orange to red, and then to deep shades of purple.

"Ya know," Cockroach said. "It's real beautiful out here. Guess this is why Butch was always dreamin' about runnin' away to sea."

Lauren watched him for a moment. "And you, where did you dream of running away to?" she asked.

Cockroach laughed quietly. "Me? I just dreamed about runnin' away, didn't make no difference where to, long as I could steal somethin', an' turn a buck."

"And now?"

Cockroach thought for a moment. "An' now? Well, everything considered, I ain't too unhappy about bein' here. Maybe I'm gonna be part of somethin' important. Maybe I'm gonna help settle the score with that U-boat."

As they talked, Gunner passed by, carrying the machine gun. "I gotta help him set up the chopper," Cockroach ended the conversation, and left.

Lauren watched him go and then turned her atten-

103

tion back to the final colors of twilight. "Not such a bad place to die, I suppose," she said to herself.

When Cockroach reached the bow, Gunner had already positioned their stolen machine gun just in front of the forward hatch. "I set the headspace, just like the manual showed," Gunner said, as he released the bolt and watched with satisfaction as a shell slid into the chamber.

"Yeah, that's good," Cockroach answered, and sat down on the hatch. "Hey, Gunner, I gotta ask you somethin'. It's been drivin' me crazy."

"Yeah, what?" Gunner asked without looking up.

"You ain't been actin' like no airplane lately. You feelin' okay?"

Gunner laid out another belt of ammunition. "Promise you won't tell nobody?"

"Yeah, promise."

"I just started doin' that to make the penguins think I was crazy. They don't expect you to do much if you're crazy."

Cockroach laughed and slapped him on the shoulder. "Gunner, you're a genius. I should of thought of that one myself."

"Of course," Gunner continued. "It got to be such a habit, that after we busted out, I couldn't remember to stop doing it."

The hours of darkness dragged slowly by as they sailed toward the coast. The wind was light and clouds gathered in the eastern sky. A soft, gray mist rose from the sea. It was near midnight before they dropped most of the sails and *Southwind* ghosted in between the two small islands. As the last sail was lowered, Stanley spun the wheel, turning the schooner's bow into the wind and bringing her to a stop. The islands were dark. Only a few tiny pinpoints of light marked houses on the distant shore. There was no sign of a U-boat.

Butch took the binoculars and climbed up to the

crow's nest. Minutes dragged by and became hours as he scanned first the sea, and then the shore, but saw only darkness.

"Dang it all," Slug grumbled from the deck below. "He ain't comin'."

"So what do we do now?" Tadpole asked.

"We wait!" Stanley answered sharply. "We wait." And so, they waited. Slug dozed on the deck, and Maisy kicked him when he started snoring. Tadpole sat by the railing, wiping his rifle with an oily dish rag again and again.

Only Sparks remained busy. As the others watched, he carried one of the radios up on deck and got Gunner to help him put it into the tender. Then he brought out a couple of the batteries and wired them together with the radio. Again, he disappeared below deck.

In the crow's nest, Butch was wiping moisture off his binoculars when he felt Maisy climb up beside him.

"So, you see anything yet?" she asked. Her voice sounded a little nervous.

"Naw, nothin'."

"Hey, Butch," she said after a moment, "look, I'm real glad you let me tag along on this."

"Why? Everything's got all messed up."

Maisy twisted a lock of her hair. "Well, because — I think — I think I really like you a lot and — well, you know." She smiled and then looked away as Butch turned suddenly to face her.

"I never said nothin' back at the orphange," he stammered, " 'cause the guys would laugh at me if I had, but I always thought you were a — well, a — a real gutsy broad."

Maisy looked up smiling. "Yeah, no kiddin'?"

Long ago, Butch had sworn that he would never kiss a girl, but at the moment he was seriously considering it. His arm fell casually across her shoulder, and he started to move his face closer when he saw a light flash. He blinked and looked again at the distant shore. The tiny light flashed again — once, twice, three times.

"Hey, look," he said in barely a whisper, "over there."

"Huh?" Maisy asked, opening her eyes, and looking where he pointed, just as the light blinked again. "Yeah, I see it."

"A signal, maybe?" he said. "Maybe someone's signaling from shore?" Quickly, he turned his eyes toward the sea, half-expecting to see the U-boat, but there was only the misty darkness. He focused his glasses on the shoreline. The strange light did not flash again, but now there seemed to be a bit of shadow, becoming longer and moving away from the shore. A streak of white glowed beside the shadow, and suddenly he knew exactly what it was.

"I think there's a speedboat heading out from shore. I can see his bow wave!" he called down to the deck.

"A speedboat?" Stanley said excitedly. "That's it! I bet he's coming out to meet the U-boat!"

Again, Butch called from the crow's nest, "But I don't see no U-boat — wait! There he is!" A few hundred yards away, the ocean began to bubble like soup on a hot stove. Maisy gripped his arm as they watched the U-boat's knifelike bow break the surface in the middle of a circle of bubbling ocean.

"I gotta go," Maisy said and suddenly kissed him. "You be careful."

"This is it!" Stanley shouted and started *Southwind*'s engine. The schooner began to move forward, slowly picking up speed with each turn of her propellers.

Just then, Sparks came running onto the deck with a look of complete panic in his eyes. "We can't do it!" he yelled. "It won't work. I can't set off the charges from the tender!"

For a moment, they all stared at him, but Stanley

106

kept steering for the U-boat's distant silhouette, and no one suggested stopping him.

"Lauren!" Cockroach called, looking around. "Get into the tender. Lauren, where are you?" At last, he saw her kneeling near the stern and hurried to her. "Quick, you gotta go," he said and then stopped short. The tender was nowhere in sight. Lauren stood up slowly. In one hand she held a knife, and in the other was a short piece of the rope which had held the tender.

"I'm sorry," she said. "But I must stay."

18

For a moment Cockroach stared blankly at Lauren as she stood at the stern, and then realized that this was no time to discuss her reasons for cutting loose the tender. "Come on," he said, "get under cover somewhere. I gotta help get the sails up."

"I'll help too," Lauren said and followed him forward to the mainmast. Butch had scrambled down from the crow's nest and was already there when they arrived. Together they raised *Southwind*'s main and foresail. The schooner dipped her rail and shot forward as the sails caught wind.

From off the starboard bow, the speedboat suddenly loomed out of the mist. For a second it looked as though the two boats would collide, but the speedboat managed to veer away at the sight of the charging schooner. A spotlight flooded *Southwind*'s decks with blinding light. For a moment it shone directly on the Coast Guard flag flying proudly from *Southwind*'s stern, and then the speedboat erupted with a hail of machine-gun fire. The first burst was high and punched a few dozen neat little holes in the mainsail.

"Hey! He's shootin' at us!" Slug yelled as he tried to dig a hole in the deck.

"Yeah, wise guy, no foolin'?" Maisy answered sarcastically and leveled her rifle across the cabin top. She fired and, as if by magic the spotlight went out with a distant tinkling of breaking glass.

Another hail of bullets tore into the cabin, and sent splinters flying across the deck. Cockroach ran for the bow as machine gun fire nipped at his heels. In a last effort he dove behind the forward hatch, just as Gunner finally got his machine gun working right. An arcing line of blood-red tracers streaked out into the night as he fired. For the speedboat, the game had suddenly changed. No longer was it facing a couple of slow-firing rifles. It veered sharply away, and began to zigzag.

"Shoot lower," Cockroach coached. "There, that's better! Now aim in front of him a little more!" Gunner held down the trigger as a long string of tracers slammed into the speedboat. Suddenly it turned, wildly out of control, and headed straight for *Southwind*.

"I think he's gonna hit us," Gunner yelled as he held down on the machine gun's trigger.

"Let's get out of here!" Cockroach ordered. He and Gunner dove down the forward hatch. A half-second later the speedboat hit and burst into flames. A piece of the bow, with the windshield and part of the fuel tank still attached, skidded across the deck, burning as it went. The rest of the hull was nothing but a ball of flame. It rolled slowly over and vanished in a cloud of steam and bubbles as the schooner ran it down.

A stream of burning gasoline spread across *Southwind*'s bow and followed Cockroach and Gunner down the hatch. There, it quickly set fire to the crew's quarters. Flames were dancing on the floor behind them when they slammed the door shut and ran aft, through the galley.

"We got fire down below!" Cockroach yelled as he burst out onto the deck.

"It doesn't matter," Stanley said calmly. He gritted his teeth and stared straight ahead, but there were tears on his cheek. The U-boat was directly in front of them, and very close. Its diesel engines screamed, as it tried to turn and move away. Men were on her foredeck, manning the big deck gun and swinging it toward the schooner as it bore down on them. Smoke billowed from *Southwind*'s hatches as the fire below spread quickly through her wooden timbers.

A blinding flash of light followed by a blast of hot air knocked Butch to his knees, as he realized that the deck gun had fired. Sails and rigging were falling all around him. Something hit him and he looked up. The schooner's main mast was gone, sheared off a few feet above the deck. Stanley was still at the wheel, although now his face was blackened and bleeding. The U-boat was only a few yards away now. *Southwind*'s bowsprit was pointed at the deck gun, and the gun crew was running, trying to get out of the way. Two of them fell into the water.

So this is it, Butch thought. *This is what it's like to die.*

One hundred tons of burning schooner struck the U-boat just forward of the conning tower. Her own momentum carried her bow up, onto the deck, and drove her bowsprit into the side of the conning tower.

Butch waited for the explosion that would finish everything. Surely now, with fire raging below *Southwind*'s decks, the charges would explode at any moment.

Maisy was suddenly crouching beside him. "Look!" she shouted, and pointed. "There's some kinda rubber boat!"

Butch raised his head and, yes, there was a rubber

life raft tied to the U-boat's rear deck. "They musta planned to use it if the speedboat didn't show up," he said and got to his feet. "Cover me, I'll try to get it."

"I'm right behind ya," Cockroach said, following him.

"Go!" Maisy yelled and fired at a figure moving on the U-boat. Butch made a dash across the deck and climbed out over the schooner's railing. As he dropped to the U-boat's deck, his feet slipped on the wet steel and he grabbed at a ladder on the side of the conning tower. Bullets began to whine all around him. A figure wearing a coat and big boots stepped suddenly in front of him, raised some sort of a club, and then fell dead.

"I got one!" Tadpole yelled. "I got one!"

Cockroach tapped him on the shoulder, and Butch saw that he had a grenade in one hand. "Go for the raft." He grinned. "I'm gonna put this down his hatch!"

Butch could see the raft, a few yards ahead of him on the U-boat's deck. He crouched low and started running just as a bullet whined over his head. He dove head first and slid into the raft. Getting to his knees, he tried to push it off into the water before he realized that it was still tied to the deck. "No knife!" he cursed and started untying the line.

A shadow fell across him. "You will not need that," a cold voice said, and Butch looked up into the barrel of Von Sturm's automatic. The world seemed to go into slow motion as the pistol was aimed between his eyes.

So close, Butch thought, *we came so close!*

A terrible scream ripped the night. He saw Slug standing on *Southwind's* railing and holding onto a rope which appeared to be attached to the tip of the foremast. "I don't wanna do this!" Slug wailed as he jumped from the rail and swung across toward the U-boat. Von Sturm looked around only in time to catch both of Slug's feet in his face. "Remember me, sucker?" Slug yelled. The pistol

111

rattled from his hand as Von Sturm was knocked head-first across the deck, and into the dark sea.

With all the grace of a five-hundred-pound pelican, Slug landed on the deck and rolled into the life raft.

"Move it, move it!" Cockroach was yelling at them as he jumped from the conning tower. "We ain't got all night!" Behind him, orange flame shot up from the conning tower hatch, as somewhere below, the grenade exploded. The U-boat shuddered and the deck began to tip. At last they pushed the raft into the water and dove in after it.

"Jump for it, now!" Butch yelled toward the schooner. With their hands and feet they all three paddled furiously toward *Southwind*'s wrecked hull, as it lay nearly on its side with the bowsprit stuck like a spear into the conning tower railing. Smoke poured from the main hatchway, and flames were spreading quickly across her foredeck as the raft approached the schooner's stern.

Butch tried to count heads as Tadpole hit the water beside him, and then Maisy. Gunner was already there.

"Is everybody away?" Stanley yelled down from *Southwind*'s stern.

"Lauren! Where's Lauren?" Cockroach demanded.

Stanley looked around. "I don't see her. I thought she already jumped!"

Maisy was holding on to the side of the raft as she wiped her hair out of her eyes. "Oh, no!" she said suddenly and pointed to *Southwind*'s deck. "There she is!"

Lauren was standing calmly by the wheel, looking into the flames which inched ever closer and closer toward her. Maisy let go of the raft and started to swim back toward the schooner.

"Stay here," Cockroach yelled, grabbing her collar and pulling her back. "I'll get her!" Before anyone could stop him, he was gone out of the raft and up over *Southwind*'s stern. He passed Stanley, who had already started for her. "Get outa here!" Cockroach told him and shoved him against the rail. Gasping for breath, Cockroach stopped in front of Lauren, and faced her. "Come on," he said as calmly as he could. "We did it. We got the sub, but we gotta go now."

Lauren shook her head, "No." Cockroach's first thought was to punch her in the mouth and carry her off. He had seen Humphrey Bogart do it in a movie once, but then he suddenly remembered that Humphrey Bogart could swim, and he could not.

"Okay, we're going, Lauren," he said, still trying to sound calm. "And you gotta help me, 'cause I can't swim a stroke." He grabbed at her arm and pulled her toward the rail.

"No!" she screamed in his face and tried to hit him as he grabbed her legs and rolled her over the side.

"I sure hope this works," he said to himself as he jumped in after her. Dark water covered him as he kicked wildly, trying to find the surface. For an instant, his head broke water. "I told you I can't swim!" he managed to yell and then went down again. With failing strength, he fought his way to the surface once more. He saw Lauren's face for only a second before he got a mouthful of water and sank again. He felt a hand on his shirt, pulling him back up. Lauren was holding him, pulling him slowly, as she swam through the water and away from the burning ships. He heard familiar voices, and other hands were pulling him up and into the raft.

For one last fleeting moment, they saw the two ships locked together and lighted by the dancing flames which swept over *Southwind*. And then the charges in her bow exploded. For an instant, night became day. The blast rocked the life raft, and showered them all with pieces of wood. The U-boat rolled slowly over on its side and began to sink. *Southwind* floated for a few more minutes as the fire engulfed her completely. Then slowly, she broke in

113

half, turned both her bow and stern toward the starry sky, and slipped proudly beneath the sea.

For a long time no one spoke as they all sat huddled together in the raft and stared out at the spot where the two ships had been. The eastern sky was turning pink with the approach of dawn when they saw the Coast Guard cutter sweeping in from the sea. As it slowed and eased alongside the raft, a familiar, pimply-faced officer stared down at them.

"Hey, Lieutenant Pimple Face, you guys are real late," Slug called. "We got this U-boat for you — "

"Don't say anything," the lieutenant cut him off. "You hooligans are in so much trouble now, you'll all be in reform school until . . ." The lieutenant's voice trailed off and his mouth dropped open as he looked toward shore and saw the U-boat's periscopes and a bit of the conning tower still visible above the water.

In a very short time, they all found themselves aboard the cutter, wrapped in blankets and drinking hot chocolate. Two navy patrol bombers were circling the sight as the cutter headed north, toward the nearest port.

"Where do we go from here?" Tadpole asked as he stared out at the sea. "Are we going back to the orphanage, and is everything gonna be like it was before we run away?"

Butch put his arm on Maisy's shoulder. "No matter where we go from here, nothin's ever gonna be the same," he said. "We did it! We killed ourselves a U-boat without no help from nobody. Nothin's ever gonna be like it was, and none of us is ever gonna be the same again."

Glossary

aft: To the rear of a boat.

bow: The forward part of a boat or ship.

bowsprit: A spar extended forward of the bow, to which stays are attached to support the mast.

brightwork: All of the brass or chrome fittings on a boat such as the winches, cleats, or compass, which are usually kept polished.

chief petty officer: A high-ranking navy non-commissioned officer.

chopper: An old gangster term for a machine-gun.

cockpit: The well in the deck, usually aft, where a boat's wheel is located.

code book: During wartime, all ships carried books containing codes to be used in radio transmissions.

commo check: Calling another radio station to see if one's own radio is working properly.

conning tower: The portion of a submarine raised above the hull which houses the periscopes and other equipment for guiding the vessel.

Corsair: A gull-winged fighter aircraft designed to be flown off of aircraft carriers.

davits: Small arms with pulleys attached, mounted on a ship and used for hoisting and lowering a small boat.

destroyer/escort: A small warship, usually about 300 feet long, used to escort convoys of merchant ships.

Deusenberg: A large and expensive American-made automobile often owned by the very rich during the early years of the twentieth century.

drydock: A place where ships or boats are hauled out of the water for repair.

flagship: The finest or largest yacht in a yacht club. Often the yacht owned by the commodore of a yacht club.

ghost: To sail slowly with almost no wind.

Great Isaac's Light: A lighthouse on the eastern edge of the Bahama Island chain.

los: German word for "away."

luff: To head a boat into the wind so that the sails flutter and the boat comes to a stop.

magnetometer: An electronic device which can locate large concentrations of magnetic metal.

main boom: The horizontal spar or pole used to hold down and extend the bottom of the main sail.

main sail: The sail which is hoisted on a boat's main mast.

picket: A ship or airplane patrol.

port: The left side of a ship when viewed looking forward from the wheel.

porthole: A small, round window on a boat or ship.

rat lines: A rope ladder attached to a sailboat's shrouds and used to climb up the mast.

salon: The main cabin on a ship or boat.

schooner: A sailing vessel that generally has two masts, with the main mast aft of a smaller foremast.

shroud: A wire which supports the mast from the port and starboard sides.

skipjack: A type of shallow-draft working sailboat used to dredge oysters.

sonar: An electronic device which uses sound waves to locate submarines underwater.

SOS: International distress signal. Originally a Morse code abbreviation for "Save our ship."

squall: A small but sometimes violent rain storm or shower.

starboard: The right-hand side of a ship when viewed looking forward from the wheel.

stern: The rear parts of a boat or ship.

tender: Usually a small rowboat, carried aboard a larger vessel, to be used for such things as getting ashore when anchored, making repairs, etc.

watch: Usually a four-hour period of duty, into which the day is divided aboard ship.

wheelhouse: An enclosed area from which a ship is steered.

U-boat: A German submarine.

yacht: Any boat used for pleasure or racing.